IVORY LIES

Carol Cail

A KISMET® Romance

METEOR PUBLISHING CORPORATION
Bensalem, Pennsylvania

Thanks to my friends who know write from wrong: Catherine, Corinne, Doris, Eileen, Sandy, Theresa.

CAROL CAIL

Carol Cail has been writing since before she could print—she dictated poems to her tolerant mother to commit to paper. The author did her own illustrations. She grew up to teach school, mother two sons, and help her husband run an office supply store in Colorado. Her publications include novels, short stories and poetry. She intends to continue writing until she forgets the words.

PROLOGUE

"How soon can this Ivan fella get out here?" The old man pressed his ear to the receiver of a phone the color and texture of an unwaxed black automobile. "Well, of course I'm doing all right, but it sure wouldn't hurt to have an extra hand around," he snarled, scissoring his bony shins impatiently under four layers of blankets on the Victorian bed.

An orange kitten sailed onto the foot of the bed and began wading the length of it, miniature knees buckling against the treacherous surface.

Another question buzzed down the telephone line, and the old man answered. "No, no problems. At least none you can help me with. My granddaughter took it into her head to come visit at Christmas, but I thought up the perfect means of keeping her away. I told her she's not to show herself here again till she's a married woman."

The kitten staggered onto the man's chest and kneaded at his once-blue nightshirt. His big hand enveloped her and massaged her matchstick ribs.

"See, this girl—woman—is one of those newfangled

libbers. Career is all she cares about. The last thing she wants is a husband, and the very last thing she wants is kids. So I got her over a barrel when I tell her to take her pick between marriage and being disowned. She'll leave us alone, I guar-en-tee you.''

A north wind broadsided the house, shivering the windowpanes.

"No, no, the hell with that. I'm happy without a family slobbering over me, you know that.'' Shifting the telephone receiver to the opposite ear while he reached to turn the alarm clock more square, he nodded automatically to the caller's tiny words. The kitten mewed a protest at being let go.

"Yeah, maybe someday I'll tell her the truth.'' The old man leaned toward the bedside stand, ready to hang up. "No! I told you before, I don't like dogs. Don't send any damn fool watchdogs. You just send me Ivan."

ONE

"Ms. Parish, we are not a callboy service."

"Mr.—" April tipped the fake walnut nameplate on the desk in front of her to check his name "Mr. S. Ruby, I am not in the market for a callboy. I am in need of a husband. For about two weeks. Till January second, to be exact."

They sat on opposite sides of the slovenly desk: a slender, well-groomed woman and a big, mussed-looking man.

"You want to hire a husband. In name only." S. Ruby abruptly dropped the letter opener he'd been toying with and peered angrily at his thumb.

"Of course, in name only," April answered coldly. She tilted her chin and sighted down her nose at him. "Someone tall."

Mr. Ruby ran a wide hand through his light brown hair, trying to lean back in his swivel chair in the cramped little screened-off space that he probably called his office. He could certainly use a larger work area; he had the impressively broad shoulders and chest of a football player. But not, apparently, a broad mind.

April had chosen this employment service at random and Mr. Ruby's cubicle the same way. Shortly after she'd settled down to tell him why she was here, the rest of the interviewing staff had trooped out en masse, loudly discussing lunch.

Well, he could damn well make up his mind there'd be no lunch for him till he found her the man she needed. April deliberately peeled off her black leather gloves and unbuttoned her black wool coat and settled deeper into the orange, hard plastic chair.

"We don't handle out-of-work actors. You need to go to a talent agency." He established eye contact and smiled.

It was a very nice smile full of hope and white, even teeth. April knew exactly what he was thinking: *Please go away, Ms. Weirdo.*

Hardening her heart, she recrossed her long legs and transferred a wisp of lint from her charcoal skirt to Mr. Ruby's battered linoleum floor. "I don't want an actor. I did try a talent agency first, and aside from the fact they wanted outrageous sums for no honest work, the actors I interviewed were all conceited or slow-witted or both. Most of them panicked at the thought of ad-libbing the entire role."

His smile had died a natural death by now. Steepling fingers to chin, he grunted, "Back up to where you said 'no honest work.'"

"I just meant it would be easy," she snapped. "It's nothing illegal. If you agree to help me with this, I'll explain the entire situation."

He studied her with a grave, steady stare that reminded her of a favorite but strict art teacher evaluating her work. "Have you had lunch, Ms. Parish?"

Now we're getting somewhere, she thought. The best bargains are always made over lunch.

"No, I haven't," she said aloud, rewarding him with the slightest curl of her lower lip.

He rattled open a desk drawer and produced one thermos, one apple, and one sandwich-shaped foil package. Rustling open the latter, he ripped the bread in two and offered her one ragged half. Peanut butter oozed out the sides.

She was so surprised she accepted it. And immediately began to look for a place to lay it down. A wastebasket would be perfect. Meanwhile, her host had twisted onto one hip to extract a pocket knife. Chopping the apple open, he extended half toward her on the tip of the blade.

"No. Thank you. Now, Mr. Ruby—"

"Call me Semi," he said, unscrewing the thermos and pouring what smelled like coffee and looked like motor oil into the thermos cap.

"Sammy—" she began again.

"Not Sammy. "Sem-eye. S-E-M-I. Coffee?"

"No. Semi—" She frowned and, distracted by the unusual name, took a bite of the sandwich.

"Sho," he said around the generous bite of apple. "Exchsplain the job."

"I have one living relative, my maternal grandfather. He's in his late eighties and dying." Everything up to the last word was true. *But everyone's dying—right?*

Semi's sympathetic smile signaled April she was wise to take this approach. Mirroring his expression, she carried on.

"Hack has a farm north of Columbus that he never leaves. I spent most of my growing-up years there, and I love the place. Love it." She could feel her face softening into a real smile, the way it always did when she thought of The Shelter. "Since I moved here to Dayton, I haven't run up there as often as I'd like. Hack doesn't encourage company. He's a little—" She bit into the sandwich again, looking for a polite word. "Eccentric."

"Uh-huh." Semi pondered "eccentric" while he wadded a sheet of typing paper and used it to scrape peanut butter off his blue-and-gold-striped tie.

"So I was going to drive up to spend Christmas with Hack whether he liked it or not. But when I phoned to tell him, he was impossible. Just impossible." Not being above a threat of tears to strengthen her case, April dabbed a knuckle suggestively below each eye. Her feelings really had been hurt by Hack's snowplow diatribe.

Semi's thoughtful stare made her wriggle straighter in the rock-hard chair. Realizing she'd eaten all but two bites of the sandwich, she popped the remainder into her mouth and dusted her hands.

When she could speak again, she said, "Listen, are you going to help me? Because if you aren't, there isn't any use discussing my private business. You put up or I shut up."

Semi Ruby was finding himself intrigued. The lady was obviously independent, cool, and tough. Bossy, no question. But he'd always lived around and liked bossy females. He knew they usually acted that way to cover endearing vulnerabilities. And she could talk as tough as she wanted, the shape of her mouth was sweet and sexy as all get-out.

"Let me see if there's anybody in my file that even fits your requirements," he said. "You go on with your story. What did your grandfather say?" Semi tucked the last of the apple into his mouth before rummaging through file folders in a wire basket labeled ACTIVE.

"He said—" April's voice roughened in a fair imitation. " 'Nobody's getting any younger and *you* sure aren't getting any smarter, April Lynn. It's time I laid down the law. Either you come to your senses and get a husband and start making me some heirs, or don't ever show your face around here again.' "

Pausing in his paper shuffling, Semi gazed at her and shook his head. "Wow, that's pretty strong."

"Right. But so am I. I'm not getting married because of a bullying old man. I'm not getting married, period."

"Yeah? You like the singles scene that much?"

Ignoring him, April rooted in her purse for a tissue to clean her hands.

"So you want a pretend husband to go to the farm with you over Christmas. To make your grandfather happy without making you unhappy."

"Someone tall," she repeated.

"And dark and handsome, I suppose? We aren't allowed to ask for physical descriptions on résumés. Not even age." He looked up from the questionnaires and grinned at her. "Where are you going to go in nine months to rent a baby?"

She scowled.

"How tall?" he asked, scanning and discarding several pages.

"I'm six feet," she said, bracing for whatever dumb remark this revelation would inspire.

"And you wear it well," he said in the same preoccupied tone.

"Oh. Thanks." April squinted over her shoulder at the deserted room. "Say, do you think there's someone else in this office who could be of more assistance?" Being around Semi was like standing one-footed on a balance beam—interesting but a little unsettling.

He glanced up, apparently surprised by this aspersion on his helpfulness, and didn't dignify it with an answer. After more shuffling of papers, he said, "I have a man coming in to take a typing test tomorrow who might do. He's looking for retail sales. As I recall, he came to about here on me.''

Standing to demonstrate, Semi held the flat of one hand to the bridge of his nose. Then he circled the desk and motioned April to stand, too. She was bemused to find that in addition to a shirt and tie, he was wearing navy sweatpants and high-top gym shoes.

Annoyed with herself for feeling embarrassed, she let him position her under his measuring hand, face-to-face. She was conscious of her smooth bangs catching in his beard stubble, and of the scent of peanut butter on his breath. Next to this bear of a man, April experienced the rare—and unquestionably pleasant—sensation of feeling small.

"Height seems okay. This applicant might be the guy you're looking for," Semi said, letting her step back and catching her arm when she did so with more haste than grace.

"Has he got references from previous employers?" she asked briskly as she brushed off his grip.

"Yes, but none from previous wives." He handed her the employment application to examine.

"Gabriel Meldon. Okay. When should I come back?"

"His appointment is one o'clock tomorrow. You can appraise him then." Hands clasped behind him, he watched her struggle with her tangled coat.

As April Parish's bootheels faded down the outer hall, Semi checked his watch. Still time to get in a few laps. He worked loose his tie, unbuttoned his shirt, and whipped both off. Taking a hooded sweatshirt out of the top drawer of his file cabinet—E for exercise—he strode toward the main hall door. Twelve steps to the fire stairway. The metal risers rang as he pelted to the top and onto the roof.

Blotches of snow, gray with age, cluttered the gravel-

and-asphalt rooftop, as did an assortment of vent pipes and a swamp cooler swathed in dirty plastic. One pigeon flapped into the dingy Ohio sky ahead of Semi as he settled into his jogger's pace, around and around the long, narrow roof. He could see his own path beginning to bore into the dusty surface, now that he'd been on this fitness kick for almost a month, since his thirty-fifth birthday.

Turning thirty-five had worried him as much as some people grieve about reaching forty. Here he was, on the sill of middle age, and what did he have to show for it? A couple of years' seniority at a so-so paying job where he could probably become office manager if he outplodded everyone else. A room of his own in his sister's warm household. His health and his sense of humor.

On his birthday, in his birthday suit, he'd looked into a full-length mirror for the first time in months—really studied himself—and realized that he'd gained too many pounds. He'd always been big, but muscle-and-bone big. If he didn't apply the brakes to his careless slide now, he might become fat.

So the dieting and exercising had begun. He'd lost five pounds and gained some self-respect.

Semi had always had friends of both sexes. Now he was noticing every female from a different perspective. Five more pounds, he'd promised himself, and then he'd actively begin searching for a wife. Someone to enjoy the better of his life before it got worse!

Take April Parish, for instance. He snorted once, thinking about the waste of time pursuing her would be. Her and her obsession about staying single.

Semi's breath came in white puffs as his knees pistoned. Sounds of traffic floated up from three stories below, and many blocks distant a siren howled. After twenty laps, he bobbed to a stop on the south side, facing the sun and, a quarter mile away, the sluggishly moving Miami River.

Her eyes were that color, like rich, muddy water, but he doubted she'd consider that a compliment.

Surprised to find himself still thinking of April Parish, Semi rubbed at a twinge of pain under his rib cage. A guy shouldn't eat before working out.

I shouldn't have let her charm me into treating her to lunch.

I shouldn't have let him bully me into sharing his lunch, April was thinking as she burped politely into her fist. Her slush-splattered black Honda hissed along a residential street a few minutes from her own.

She'd lived in Dayton for three years, in the same apartment for two years, by herself for one year. Her last roommate—female—loved rap music, hated housecleaning, and still owed April two hundred dollars, and she'd been the best roommate in a dreary series. Determined to live alone, April had whittled her clothes and entertainment budgets to pay for the luxury.

Some of her rent could be deducted from income tax because she worked at home as a freelance artist. She occupied the top floor of a turn-of-the-century, brick, foursquare house near Union Station. At thirty-one, she was modestly successful in her career and, as she liked to put it, happily unmarried.

And Grandfather Hackett wasn't going to browbeat or con her into changing that. She had no qualms about conning him, however, into thinking he'd won.

What did worry her was his sudden eruption of unreasonableness after so many years of smoldering perversity. He'd always been cantankerous, but his threatening to disinherit her was downright mean. He hadn't seemed very interested in her job or her love life till now. Maybe he *was* dying. Maybe he'd been diagnosed with a terminal disease that made him anxious to settle her affairs as well as his own.

Biting her lip with this new worry, April aimed the car into an ice-streaked space by the curb only half a block from home.

Even if Hack hadn't been her *only* relative, he'd have been her *favorite* relative. She hoped to be just like him when she was old—strong and self-reliant and full of ginger.

At least he had been like that until now. How awful, if he was seriously ill.

Yanking up the emergency brake, April rested a hand on the door handle, still preoccupied with thoughts of Hack. Maybe he wasn't sick at all. Maybe he had decided he could trick her into doing something he'd always been nagging her to do—to get married—by feigning bad health. It was the kind of lie she herself knew how to tell, a tactful lie to smooth out human relationships. A darker shade of white.

Laughing out loud, she gathered up her purse and swung both feet into the sloppy-cold street. Here she was going to all the trouble of hiring a hand in marriage, and the one person who would fully appreciate and understand the scheme was the very man she couldn't tell—the old man she was duping.

Slamming shut the car door, she slip-slid around to the sidewalk and picked her way along it toward the house.

If this were a forties' movie, the retail salesman Semi Ruby was lining up for her would turn out to be Cary Grant or John Wayne, and she'd fall madly in love and take back everything she'd said about staying single.

Fat chance!

Semi Ruby stepped up on Your Accurate Weight and Actual Fortune scales in the main-floor vestibule and stood patiently while the indicator settled down. He'd lost another pound. Tipping his head at the chrome wall behind, he ran the flat of his palm from forehead to hair, examining the line of demarcation. And groaned.

The gray cardboard fortune read, "You have two choices: Take it or leave it."

Twenty-four hours later, April stood beside Mr. Ruby's scruffy desk, shaking hands with her prospective employee, Gabriel Meldon, who didn't look like Grant or Wayne. He reminded her more of a Nordic Tom Selleck—tall, light, and handsome. April smiled politely, thinking, *So far, so good*.

Turning to Semi Ruby, she felt the smile warm. He was wearing a blue shirt and a navy tie—a good match for the sweatpants. She wasn't sure why she was pleased to see him, unless it was because he'd found her a pseudo-husband.

"Coffee?" he suggested, hovering a hand over the plaid thermos on the desk.

"Just say no," she cautioned Mr. Meldon.

"Want to sit down, then?" Semi continued to play host.

She hadn't noticed before what a becoming tan his face had. She wanted to ask how he had got it this time of year.

Instead, she said, "The chairs are as awful as the refreshments, but, yes, let's sit."

Everyone eased down carefully, avoiding bumping long legs on the desk or one another.

Semi shuffled through papers and read from one. 'Mr. Meldon is between jobs right now. His training and experience are in sales.'

"What have you sold, Mr. Meldon?" April asked in her best throaty alto. She shrugged off the black coat and smoothed the skirt of a red dress.

"Call me Gabe." His voice was deep and hinted of a Southern drawl. "Used cars. Office supplies. Drugs."

"Drugs?"

"Prescription."

"Oh."

"The good kind."

"Of course."

Semi, suddenly feeling like a chaperon and hating it, interrupted his clients' growing rapport by knocking a phone book onto the floor.

"Would you like to explain your job opportunity to Mr. Meldon, Ms. Parish?" he asked, sorry for making her jump.

She cleared her throat. "Surely. Well. It isn't a sales position." For some unaccountable reason, she found herself reluctant to go on. Glancing at Semi, thinking his encouraging smile was more like a smirk, she said to Gabe, "I need someone to pose as my husband for two weeks, beginning a week from today. He would have to be able to go with me to visit a relative in central Ohio."

The glint of interest in Gabe's pastel blue eyes intensified. "And what, exactly, would be the duties?"

"Just companionship," she said airily. "Platonic. Companionship."

Gabe looked from her to Semi and back. "Companionship. How much does it pay?"

"Considering it amounts to a paid vacation for you, all expenses and forty dollars a day," she said with more hope than confidence. "It'll be over in two weeks and you can get a real job."

"Just between you and me, April," Gabe said, inaccurately, "am I the first guy you've tried to hire?"

"What difference does that—"

"You've got about five days to find someone, not counting the weekend. You're asking this someone to spend Christmas with you instead of his own family. Seems like you might want to pay the right man more than minimum wages.''

When she glanced at Semi again, he shrugged unhelpfully. April raised her chin and her voice. ''Perhaps forty, expenses, and a bonus afterward.''

''Mmm-hmm, a bonus,'' Gabe put on a show of considering. ''Sort of like Most Valuable Player?'' His lazy smile had to have been practiced daily in a mirror, it was that good.

Semi abruptly leaned toward them, banging his knees on the hollow-sounding desk. ''Can we assume your wife wouldn't object to your taking this job?''

''We can ask her.'' Gabe winked deliberately at April. ''Whenever I get a wife.''

''All expenses, a bonus, and fifty dollars a day,'' she bid recklessly.

Her potential employee consulted the toes of his cowboy boots for ten seconds. ''It's crazy, but what the heck. I'll do it,'' he decided, offering his hand on it and holding hers a bit longer than necessary.

''Good,'' she said, beaming at Semi before giving Gabe her full attention again. ''Let me have your address and phone number, and I'll pick you up next Friday evening for the drive north.''

''Shouldn't we have dinner before then so you can fill me in on my role?'' He expanded his smile a notch broader.

''That really isn't necessary. We're newlyweds who don't know much about each other. Besides, I can tell you more than you want to know on the way to Grandfather's.''

''How about Italian? You like Italian? Or Chinese? French? You say, and I've got the perfect restaurant for it.''

Semi's chair squealed as he tipped back, arms folded,

and gave April a squinty-eyed look that reminded her of Hack.

"Well, okay, maybe it would be a good idea to have one date before the marriage," she said.

Gabe issued a delighted, husky rasp of a laugh.

Putting their heads together, literally, over Semi's dog-eared desk calendar, April and Gabe agreed on Thursday at seven at an Italian cafe near the Convention Center. He gripped her hand again and left, with backward smiles that indicated he'd be counting the hours.

"You did it," April rejoiced, pulling on her coat and reaching her hand across the desk to seal their business together.

Semi drew her hand between both of his, like a moth he'd caught and didn't want to crush. "You aren't afraid to drive into the country with a total stranger?"

Ordinarily, she'd be squirming to be free of this unwanted, too personal contact. But, feeling pleased with herself and, by extension, with Semi Ruby, she tolerated the awkward position of leaning across his hard-edged desk. His big hands were warm and dry and oddly reassuring.

"Gabe won't be a total stranger," she said. "I mean, we'll get acquainted some on Thursday. And, of course, he knows that you know who I'm with."

"Of course I know! It makes me feel like an accessory or a pimp or something."

Embarrassed, she twitched out of his grip and grabbed her coat. "We're just easing the mind of an old man by telling him what he wants to hear. Everyone should be as solicitous of their elders." She began to squeeze buttons into buttonholes the length of her coat.

"I have some paperwork here for you to sign," Semi said, slapping it down on her side of the desk.

She signed extravagantly, overrunning the lines. "It's such a relief to have found a man."

"I bet." His expression, when she checked it, was carefully blank. "Here's my card. In case you think of anything more I can do. Wait." He jerked it back and scribbled on it. "That's my home number—should you need a brother or a cousin on short notice."

First she glared, then she had to laugh. She stowed the card into a coat pocket and picked up her gloves.

Semi relaxed backward in his noisy chair, his hands clasped behind his head. "What line of work are you in, Ms. Parish?"

"Why?"

"Just curious. You love your work, you said."

"Commercial art. I illustrate children's books and magazines."

"Oh, yeah, I can see how that could be a real pleasure. I like kids myself."

"I don't actually like children per se," she corrected. "I'm not around them much. Drawing bunnies and fire engines is what I enjoy." Shoving the shoulder bag into place, she scraped the orange chair out of her way, raising her voice as she backed off. "Thanks again."

"My job," he said, scrambling to his feet, smoothing the hairs on the nape of his neck. "Be careful, hear?"

She clip-clopped out and he settled back into his chair, trying to decide whether the trailing perfume was musk or some kind of flower. He was afraid he was catching a cold; he suddenly felt so *down*.

Semi's depression persisted—though the cold didn't materialize—right up to eleven-thirty on Thursday night, when the phone on his nightstand rang. Tenting his library book of Western fiction over his stomach, he hoisted the receiver.

"Mr. Ruby?" April Parish's crisp voice made him

struggle straighter against the pillows. "We have a problem."

"What? What!" Across the room, his reflection in the closet mirror wore twisted pajamas and a worried look.

"Gabriel Meldon. He's not working out. He's just—" She drew a breath that seemed to suck the receiver away from his head. "Awful."

"Awful?" He switched to his other ear. "Are you all right?"

"Could you come over right away? I don't know where else to turn."

"Of course," he soothed, stirring the night table for pen and paper. "How about the police?" he added practically.

"I don't want the police!"

"Shh, okay. Doctor?" He clicked a ballpoint at the ready.

"You. Just you." If she'd said it with a little less snarl, he'd have been thrilled.

"Where are you, April, do you know?" he asked with his best guidance counselor's inflection.

"I'm at home." Her answer should have frosted his eardrum. "I believe if I concentrate really hard, I can recall what the address is for you."

He wrote it down, nodding and mmm-hmming. "Be there in half an hour. I'll knock once, pause, and knock three times."

"I'll try to stay awake for it," was her sarcastic exit line.

TWO

Rap. Pause. Rap, rap, rap.

He shifted from foot to rubber-booted foot, looking around the tiny landing outside April Parish's apartment. Hers was the only door on this upper floor; the ornate walnut stairs led up to this threshold and stopped dead. The pinnacle. Or the end of the line.

She swept the door open and caught him yawning. He pinched off his gray tweed cap and stepped past her into the dimly lit cavern.

"Thank you for coming," was her rote greeting.

"No problem."

He strolled forward to study the room. White predominated, except for the black skylights and pastel paintings that trooped around all the walls.

"Sit down." She waved toward a white sectional big enough to sleep a family of four.

His rubber soles cheeped on the oak plank flooring, and the sofa sighed under his weight. She sat down on the same section six feet away and considered her manicure.

Not being a fashion expert, Semi didn't know the

name for the outfit she was wearing. It put him in mind of Arabian deserts: a beige dress, straight and low-cut and covered with embroidered mirrors. When she breathed she flashed.

"So what's the trouble?" he asked.

The dress blazed with her huge sigh. "Mr. Meldon talks. All the time. He never shuts up." She threw out her hands, appealing for sympathy. "Mostly about himself."

Semi, who'd been expecting a sorry tale of attempted rape, relaxed his backbone. "And, ummm, you don't think you could, ummm, live with that little character flaw for a few days?"

"That isn't all."

Well, sure. She'd have to build up her courage to talk about the really bad things. He smiled encouragingly at her.

"Stop smirking! I know you tried to warn me about inviting a stranger into my life." The dress winked hypnotically as she rearranged a pillow at her back.

"You want to get it off your ch—" He looked hastily away from that group of mirrors and amended his question to, "Tell me about it?"

"We had supper. Very nice. Steak and all the trimmings. Wine. Except for the fact that he talked with his mouth full, I was reasonably satisfied. So then he invited me to his place to see his arrowhead collection."

Semi groaned. "You didn't fall for that old guano."

"Of course not. I made him come up here instead."

He groaned again.

"I keep mace handy at all times," she informed him tartly. "Anyway, I wasn't worried about him trying to kiss me. He wouldn't want to tie up his mouth that long."

Gathering his legs under him, Semi stood. "Ms. Parish—April—when you called me, I thought you needed rescuing. Since you seem to be okay, I think I better—"

"I *do* need rescuing." Her glare changed to a softer expression that might even be remorse. "Please, sit down. Stay," she wheedled. "I'm sorry if I've been rude to you. Would you like some coffee?"

"No, thanks," he said, settling gingerly on the edge of the couch again. "What do you mean you need rescuing?"

"I mean he and I had a big fight and he wouldn't work for me now if I were the last employer on earth and likewise I'm sure."

"What was the fight about?" Semi's eyes darted into all the corners, searching for Gabe's dead body.

"He said—" She raised her chin a good three inches. "He made fun of my work. He called my art 'cutesy-pooh.' "

"Cutesy—" he echoed.

She nodded. "Pooh."

For several heartbeats they sat staring at each other. Then April's head bowed into her cleavage and her shoulders shook. Semi, who regarded crying women as an emergency akin to being struck by lightning, slapped himself searching for a handkerchief.

"He was such a pompous son of a—" She dissolved into a wail that was, he realized, laughter.

"Well, then—" Relieved, he tried to get her attention, smiling gamely at her humorous fit. "So what's the problem? You're lucky you found out before you got all the way to your grandfather's with him."

She straightened, hugging her waist. "I need a new husband."

"Oh. Oh, yeah." His forehead furrowed with a new train of worry as he began to guess where this conversation was leading. "I don't think there's anyone else in my files who would do." Shaking his head at the shame of it, he avoided eye contact with her. "Nobody . . . tall enough."

"You could do it," she suggested soberly. "You'd be perfect."

"Hey, no. Wait a minute—" He stood up, and she jumped into his path, bracing her hands on his chest. "I'm not good at lying—honest!" he pleaded.

"All you have to do is nod your agreement to whatever ivory lie I tell."

"Ivory?"

"It's an untruth that's a shade more creative than white," she explained, straight-faced.

"I've already got a full-time job," he croaked.

"I'll pay you sixty dollars a day." Close up, her Miami River irises contained iridescent oil slicks of gold and rose. "Please, Semi. Don't you have some vacation time you could take over the holidays?"

The natural thing to do was to close his hands around her bare forearms to steady her. The smart thing to do was to step sideways and make a beeline for the door. Compromising, he jammed his hands in his pockets and stood his ground.

"I couldn't take two weeks off, April. I really couldn't."

"Weekends, then. You can drive my car back and forth on the days you have to be at work. The trip's only about two hours one way."

He started to shake his head, and she clamped it between her palms. "If you don't say yes," she warned so low he had to lean into her to hear, "I'm going to a singles bar and hire the first guy who orders me a drink."

"You wouldn't." He squinted at her unblinking eyes. "You would."

"Wait, wait! Don't say yes yet." She grabbed his

arm and muscled him toward the far wall. "First I want to know how you'd describe my work."

She positioned him in front of a two-by-three framed watercolor of a rosy-cheeked piglet pouring tea for a tableful of assorted animal cronies. The setting was a Victorian porch during a summer shower. Rain gushing from a downspout was being ridden by a ladybug in a rubber raft.

Fingering his jaw, Semi considered. "Charming" came to mind, but that was too trite a word. April waited, impatiently drumming her fingers against her thighs.

"I know a child who would dearly love this," he said, missing her smile because he was shuffling away along the wall to view the rest.

"You have children?" She craned to see his hand, suddenly realizing that she'd been selfishly trying to manipulate his life when he might, after all, be a father, with a father's duties and pleasures at Christmastime. "I didn't think—"

"Oh, I'm not married. My sister has a lot of kids."

"Great. Well, then, you'll do this for me?" She followed him to the end of the wall.

Stalling for time, he pretended total absorption in the last picture, a sketch of a potbellied lion skateboarding, with his tail draped safely over one arm. April Parish the artist displayed a sense of fun that April Parish the woman seemed afraid to indulge.

Semi knew he ought to refuse to have any more to do with her scheme to fool her grandfather. It was too much trouble, too wild, too likely to fail. And yet April herself was the kind of intriguing woman he'd rarely had a chance to meet. Smart. Creative. Beautiful. And begging him to spend day after day with her. How could he resist?

"Will you do it?" she repeated.

Turning to peer curiously into the little galley kitchen along the intersecting wall, Semi said as easily as if it were something he'd always planned to do, "In the words of Gabriel Meldon, it's crazy, but what the heck." The rest of his acceptance speech was literally choked off by April's spontaneous hug around his neck.

Before he could get used to it, she pulled back and looked him up and down. "Do you always wear sweatpants?"

"I jog a lot," he said defensively.

"Uh-huh. When was the last time you shaved?"

"Where in the contract does it say you get to nag—"

"Give me your home address. I'll pick you up at seven tomorrow night, and you'll be meeting Grandfather Hack by ten."

"What kind of name is that—Hack?" he asked, writing obediently on the scrap of paper she provided.

"Nickname." She whisked the paper away as if afraid he'd change his mind. "And very descriptive."

The next morning, April phoned her grandfather, and as soon as they'd hung up, Hack made a call of his own. He was standing at the kitchen counter scowling at the curling wallpaper, a hand cocked on one hip, ankle-deep in cats.

Without any preliminary chitchat, Hack said, "Is Ivan on his way, and has he got what's-his-name with him?" He listened for a moment. "No, that's okay. It looks like I'm going to have family for Christmas after all, but I can handle it."

Leaning down to extract one of the kittens whose claws had penetrated his pant leg, Hack said, "My little plan to keep the grandkid away backfired. Well, hell, I can't believe April Lynn is really as married as she claims, but we'll see. 'Course, we don't know anything about this so-called groom, so that's where the danger is.''

He deposited the kitten on the countertop and spread his bony hand as a guardrail while the animal prowled. ''I sure didn't credit how much she wanted what I've got.'' The old man snorted. ''But we'll manage, don't worry.''

He hung up before the other end could say good-bye or offer any dogs.

April considered herself a capable, usually a calm sort of person, but as she drove through the city's back streets to pick up Semi Ruby, she was unquestionably nervous. What if he'd changed his mind and wouldn't go with her? What if he did go and turned out to have some really disgusting quirk of character? What if Hack couldn't stand him and took it out on her?

Turning into the designated street, she wound down the window, looking for house numbers. It was a neighborhood of clapboards and shingles, thirties' vintage houses a little the worse for wear. Some were gussied up with multicolored Christmas lights along the gables.

''Watch for the red porch,'' he'd said. She drew in at the curb and sat staring. She'd expected a barn-red or red-brick porch, not fire-engine scarlet with green dragons on the ceiling and unicorns flanking the front door. The rest of the house had been painted to resemble bouldered castle walls. Primary-colored flags fluttered from the roof.

Shaking off her fascination, she tapped the horn three times as agreed. No more than a minute passed before the front door swung inward—she'd half expected it to drop like a drawbridge—and Semi trudged out, a suitcase in each hand. She stepped out into the slush to open the hatch for him.

"Evening," he said, his breath trailing him like smoke.

"Hello again." With her arms stiff at her sides, she danced in place to the cold. "That all?" He nodded, and she slammed the lid. "I like your Christmas decorations," she called across the roof as she returned to the driver's side.

"What Christmas decorations? Oh. No, it's painted that way all the time. Be right back," he said and tramped toward the porch again.

A swoop of doubt added to her chill. Was she making a big mistake, soliciting the company of a man she didn't know? Did she really intend to spend two weeks in close proximity with a stranger who lived in a house painted like the set of a children's TV show?

Then she imagined Hack's stubborn jaw as he ordered her off his property for failure to comply with his instructions. How sad—to be turned away from the house she loved by the grandfather she loved.

This scenario having restored her resolve, April slid into the warm car, shivered one final time, and checked the heater setting. When she looked up, Semi was opening the passenger door and tipping the seat forward for someone small to climb into the back.

Dropping in beside April as she craned to see the interloper, Semi rested an arm on the seat back and smiled at everyone. "Ms. Parish, this young man is Gayner Nussman. Gayner, this is Ms. Parish. Only she's aka Mrs. Ruby this weekend."

Gayner raised one hand, fingers wiggling.

April about-faced and leaned into Semi's bulky shoulder. "What is this?" she hissed.

"It was his weekend. I didn't think you'd mind. In fact, you mentioned wanting to rent a kid."

"A baby. Grandfather's not going to believe I never

mentioned having a—what?—a ten-year-old son. What do you mean by 'his weekend'?''

"I'm sort of a big brother to my sister's tribe. They take turns going places with me on weekends."

"That's admirable. Unselfish of you and all that. But couldn't you have skipped this one and taken Gayner somewhere next weekend?" She glanced into the back-seat again, her smile sweet and short.

"Next weekend I'll be at your grandfather's, too," he reminded her, straightening around in preparation for the ride. "Gayner can be my son from a previous marriage if you want."

Rolling her eyes, April yanked the gear into drive. "Okay, just so he doesn't expose our charade." They went two blocks before she thought to add, "And he's not on my payroll."

All her doubts about what she'd got herself into came galloping back as she drove though Dayton automatically. Not only a strange man, but also a strange child—and to April, every child was strange. She'd been trying to set up a situation that would please Hack and—coincidentally, of course—assure her inheritance. But maybe what she'd set up was a disaster.

In the relatively sparse night traffic of eastbound I-70, April flexed her arms and forced herself to relax. The dry highway hummed softly to the tires. The clear charcoal sky glittered with stars.

She cast a quick look at Semi. He'd unbuttoned his denim-and-fleece jacket to reveal a flannel shirt and jeans. He *did* look the part of a clean, intelligent, good-natured husband.

"Did you pack your sweats?" she teased.

He huffed as if it were funny.

"You want to get our story straight?" she suggested. "I'll tell you how I planned it, and you can input corrections or additions."

His clothes rustled as he twisted toward Gayner to say, "You listen, too, kiddo. Remember, this is sort of Let's Pretend, to make an old man happy."

"Exactly," April said. "So let's pretend we've been married a week and we've known each other only a couple of months. That will explain our not knowing much about each other's likes and dislikes. We were married by a justice of the peace with strangers for witnesses, a spur-of-the-moment decision."

"Grandpop's going to think you're pregnant," piped up from the rear seat.

"I'm not! He won't. I mean, the idea is we just swept each other off our feets. Feet. We're impulsive," she blustered, giving Semi a sidelong look.

His big body and bland face looked about as impulsive as a stone wall. Then he swiveled and winked at her, and the dashboard lighting chiseled it into a leer.

"Seems to me we should always stick as close to the truth as possible," he said.

"Yeah? Meaning?"

"Why not admit that you married me because you needed a husband, and I married you because of your beautiful brown eyes and high intelligence? Among other things."

Disconcerted, she forced her attention back to the highway. "Good idea."

"What other things?" Gayner wanted to know.

April overrode him. "I'll tell you about my family. Grandfather is Hackett Jones. He had one daughter, Evelyn, my mother. She died of a heart attack a couple of years ago. I can't remember Grandmother Jones at all; she died when I was a toddler. When they were first married, Hack inherited this big farm he calls The Shelter, and he's lived and worked there ever since."

Semi was watching the dark landscape out the side window, nodding slightly to show attentiveness.

"You got a father?" came from the backseat.

"Sometime, somewhere." She gritted her teeth into a smile. "He ran away from home when I was twelve. Mother and I lived with Grandfather after that." The smile softened as she thought of being *home* again.

"Chasing tail, was he?" Gayner asked in a tone of polite interest.

Thinking that she must have heard wrong, April tried to imagine what he'd really said, till he repeated it. "Because my dad did that, too," he explained. "Deserted us for a nympho."

"Well, yes." She was too flustered to deny it. "I believe there was another woman involved." April imagined her grandfather listening to this conversation. He'd probably roar at everyone to get out of his sight and then laugh about it in private. Why couldn't Gayner have been a sweet, quiet little girl?

To change the subject, April asked Semi, "Did you say your house is always painted like that?"

"No." He breathed a few times and said, "Last spring it was blue, with fish and mermaids and seaweed."

Gayner giggled.

"Why?" she wanted to know.

"Why not?" Semi kept smiling at her till she smiled. Then he said, "It's my sister's house, so I don't have much choice. I always vote for a nice conservative plaid, and I always get shouted down."

She forced her eyes back to the road, shaking her head in amazement. "You live with your sister and her—how many children?"

"How many, Gayner?" He turned to consult.

"Ten."

"Ten."

"Ten!" *That poor woman. Gayner's father had obvi-*

*ously not run off soon enough. Or, more likely, Semi's
sister had remarried.*

"I guess I need to know more about your family,
too, Semi. For *Hack's* benefit." She punched on the
speed control and prepared to be entertained. "First off,
why do you live with your sister?"

"Dale needs the rent money. And it's cheaper for
me than an apartment or something. I like being part of
one big, happy family. Enough reasons?" He sounded
amused rather than defensive.

"What's 'Semi' short for?"

"Nothing. It's my name."

"Oh, come on. That's not a name, that's a truck."

"Right. That's how I got it. As a kid, I loved trucks.
Vroom, vroom. And then in high school I *looked* like
one, so the name stuck."

Gayner wriggled on the backseat, ostentatiously holding his mouth shut on laughter.

"Well, it seems to me now that you're an adult,
you'd drop the silly nickname."

He imitated her stern tone. "Well. My real name is
even sillier."

"Middle name?" she demanded.

"None."

"Nun? Did you also like ladies in long black
dresses?"

"N-O-N-E," he spelled with mock-injured dignity.

April sniffed disdainfully. "How about if I call you
Sem? That sounds better than 'Semi.' "

From the backseat came sounds of exaggerated
gagging.

"Sure. As long as I can shorten 'April' to one sylla-
ble, too," Semi agreed cheerfully.

"Hee, hee, hee." Gayner boiled over. "Hee, hee,
hey, Stepmom, I need to go to the bathroom."

"Okay, okay. Hang on. I'll look for an exit." She

checked the rearview mirror and eased right. "And don't call me Stepmom. Or Ape."

"Gotcha. And you call me Gay and you're dead."

The truck stop at the next exit was an anthill of activity, the big rigs idling in rows, white exhaust curling their sides, their operators inside asleep or in the restaurant girding themselves with food and conversation for the next leg of the journey. Parking the compact car was like berthing a tugboat among ocean liners.

Following Semi single file through vehicles, April thought he looked at home, clothed and built like a very masculine trucker. When he pushed the restaurant door open wide for her and Gayner to precede him, she caught a whiff of aftershave, something musky, which surprised and—she couldn't say why—pleased her. She *could* say why—it was flattering that he wanted to smell that good around her!

While Gayner scouted out the rest room, April and Semi found a vacant booth with a view of the gasoline islands and ordered two coffees and a hot chocolate. April scanned the smoky, people-cluttered room before looking directly at her new husband.

Taking up more than half his side of the table, Semi had the kind of build April had always looked for and rarely found in her high school dates. She'd been painfully tall from junior high on. Though she'd always told herself that height was not the most important masculine trait, few boys were willing to date a girl who towered above them. Part of her determination to be a career woman was, she supposed, her disappointment at how often she'd encountered masculine insecurities concerning her height.

Whatever insecurities Semi harbored, they wouldn't involve size. She remembered her early impression of him as a linebacker, but now she amended that to quarterback—big, but not too big, and smart, no question.

"You were going to tell me about yourself," she said, dropping her chin on a propped hand.

He drew circles on the tabletop, grinning that smirky smile of his—an indication, she realized, of his shy streak. Impulsively, she put her hand on top of his, resting beside his steaming coffee cup.

"Thank you again, Semi. This isn't what you wanted to be doing over Christmas. I'll try to make it as pleasant as possible for you."

His eyes warming, he openly studied her face. "Actually, it will be kind of nice, getting away from the kids for a while, being in the country. Out with the cows and pigs."

"Sorry. The only kind of livestock Hack keeps anymore is cats."

He nodded at the hand she'd forgotten to withdraw. "I see I bought you a wedding ring. No diamond, though?"

"You're too cheap to pop for a stone," she said. "In fact, you bought this gold band at Kmart."

"It embarrasses me to hear it. Hope being married to you will improve my character."

Gayner wormed next to Semi in the booth, breaking up the tête-à-tête. While the boy began to lick whipped topping off his cocoa, April got her first real look at him. He didn't much resemble his uncle; thin-faced, swarthy, with big dark eyes, he bobbed and weaved in constant, nervous motion.

"What grade are you in?" she asked him, flinching as a flailing sneaker invaded her space under the table.

Gayner tunneled a hand under his Nintendo T-shirt to scratch. "You mean what year of school? Fifth. Can I have a cheeseburger?"

"You just had supper," Semi said. "April wants to get on up the road." He cupped his big hand on the back of Gayner's slender neck in a gesture of obvious affection.

Setting her empty cup aside, April rooted through her bag for change to pay the bill. "Are you the oldest, youngest, or middlest of the ten children?"

Gayner clutched his forehead with one hand and counted off on the fingers of his other. "Jo, Daffy, Desmond, Leroy, me. We're all the youngest."

"You're all the youngest?" She frowned, waiting for the punch line.

"Yeah." He picked up a spoon and made faces at his upside-down image. "We're all ten. I don't know who's the oldest ten," he added, discouraging further questioning.

"Come on. I'll explain in the car," Semi said, shrugging into his jacket.

"My sister, Dale, and her husband, William, operate a children's home," Semi said once they'd circled onto the interstate again.

"Ohhh."

"What used to be called an orphanage. A foster care arrangement. The youngsters range from ten to fifteen. At least the current crop does."

"Oh, so Gayner's not your blood nephew. You live there and help out. That's wonderful."

Actually, she thought it sounded awful. No privacy. No independence. No swinging except in the backyard.

"You got any tapes?" Gayner demanded.

"Sure. Which do you prefer? New Age or classical?"

Groaning, he slumped into the corner and began finger-painting the fogged side window.

"What about your parents?" April asked Semi. "Still living?"

"Just Mom. She lives in a retirement center in Centerville. In her seventies, but she still gets around good.

Drives a big Oldsmobile and visits us on holidays or whenever else she takes the notion. Brings the kids presents.''

"Soap and socks and junk like that," Gayner elaborated with disgust.

The moon had sailed out of fields on their right and now played peep among the ragged clouds. The tires thumped rhythmically, counting off miles and minutes.

April reached to turn down the heater fan, stealing a glance at Semi. With his chin tucked to his chest, he might be dozing. A wisp of hair marked his forehead like a soft apostrophe.

Suddenly April was sure that Hack would like this man—as well as Hack had ever liked anyone.

She thought she could like Semi a lot herself.

Back in Dayton, in a prefabricated house surrounded by architectural clones, Ralph Greene propped himself against the kitchen/laundry room doorjamb and took the final swig from his fifth can of beer before throwing it at the far wall. He was down to one clean shirt and no clean underwear. Time to *do* something.

He tacked across the kitchen floor to the wall phone, dialed three wrong numbers, and finally got the snippy voice he wanted.

"Where the hell is your sister?" he whined into the mouthpiece.

His answer was a click and a dial tone.

Turning the car onto the last stretch of gravel road, April lightly prodded Semi, who had definitely begun to quietly snore, and announced, "We're two miles from The Shelter."

Yawning, he twisted his neck to clear the cricks.

"Do we have to go to the bathroom in a whatchacallit—outhouse?'' Gayner, who'd been singing "Jingle Bells" for the past twenty miles, sounded hopeful.

"There are five bathrooms, all inside," April replied, disillusioning him.

"Five?" Semi said. "Big place."

"Yup." Instead of being tired, she was excited. She hadn't been to the homestead since early fall, and she hadn't realized how much she was looking forward to being there again.

"How many acres has your grandfather got?"

"I don't know. Two, three hundred."

Here was the crossroads where the woods began. The trees' shadows swallowed the car for a quarter mile. Coming into the moonlight again, April noted that the next landmark, a weathered wood sign, had slipped another degree out of true.

Gayner, who'd unbuckled his seat belt to hang over Semi, chortled as he read it aloud. " 'Keep out and keep breathing.' "

"I know I'm going to love this man," Semi said.

Something four-footed slunk across the road and into the ditch, turning to track them with glowing red eyes. Another gray sign loomed on a fence post.

"What's this one say?" Gayner exclaimed in April's ear. " 'Don't even think about it!' Whooo, I love it. Make my day."

"Dirty Harry hadn't been invented yet when my grandfather put up these warnings," April commented dryly. "Or I'm sure 'Make my day' would have graced one of them."

Another sign, a simple, NO TRESPASSING!!!!, and they were at the mouth of the narrow, weed-infested lane. April braked to turn, and the headlights swept the silver mailbox with HACK'S TAX SHELTER stenciled on the side.

Semi laughed. "The Shelter, huh? Gimme shelter."

April elevated her jaw and kept quiet.

Peering at a black outline of roof a city block ahead, Semi said, "Your grandfather *is* expecting us?"

"Oh, yeah. I telephoned him this morning to tell him I'd bagged a husband."

"What did he say to that?"

"Ummm, I believe his exact words were, 'If you have to come out here, I suppose you'll want to bring the bastard along.' " She bit her tongue, remembering Gayner too late as he tittered appreciatively.

The car jounced past the dark house to the barnyard, and now they could see the watery yellow illumination of the kitchen windows. April tooted the horn as she cut the motor, announcing their arrival. Semi betrayed his nervousness by buttoning and unbuttoning his jacket.

A yard light burst on overhead and the back door swung open.

"Jeeze," Gayner observed. "Is that your grandfather?"

"Yup," April said, feeling a mixture of pride and apprehension as she slammed the car door and walked to greet the old man.

Age usually warps a man, shrivels him; but Hackett Jones still stood straight and steady, all seven feet of him. His blue work shirt and overalls hung loose as a scarecrow's on his lanky, angular frame. What hair he had left was white and long, wild around his skin-and-bones face.

He looked like a geriatric Frankenstein's monster.

"Hello, Hack," April crooned, trying to hug him and missing as he stooped to pick up a tall-tailed kitten that had been massaging his legs. Two older cats leaped onto the porch and queued up to be let inside.

"Well, come in, then," Hack said with no detectable congeniality.

THREE

The big kitchen, lit by one overhead fixture missing two bulbs, was warm. In a few minutes it would be too hot, but at first it felt great. The old man clumped to the head of the claw-footed, oilcloth-covered table and set the kitten down on it beside the remains of a pizza. Drawing out a side chair, April dumped her purse on the seat, undid her coat, and smiled till it hurt.

"Hack, this is my brand-new husband, Semi Ruby. Semi, my grandfather, Hackett Jones."

Semi made a trip up the room to shake hands. "How do you do, sir?"

The two men eyed each other as if it were a contest where the first one to smile lost.

"Sam, did she say?" Hack rumbled.

"Sem," Semi corrected from long practice. "Rhymes with 'phlegm.' And an *i* on the end, rhymes with 'I.' "

Hack nodded. "You two married?"

"Oh, yeah," Semi lied gamely. "Us. Two. Uhh, married."

"Well, isn't this nice!" April rushed to say. "Home for the holidays."

42

"I don't know about 'nice.' " Her grandfather raised his voice. "I'm kind of busy right now, and I don't need company. Even you. Though I got to say I'm real relieved you finally found yourself a husband."

Wincing, April forced cheerfulness into her voice. "We won't bother you. We'll entertain ourselves. And maybe there's something we can do to help you with whatever it is you're busy doing."

Ignoring the offer, Hack said, "Who's this?" and frowned at Gayner, who immediately crawled under the table, ostensibly to pet a cat.

Hauling him out for the introduction, Semi claimed him as "my son by my first wife." Gayner fidgeted under the old man's inspection.

"Where's your mother, boy?" Hack interrogated.

His eyes showing lots of panicky white, Gayner suffered an uncharacteristic loss of words. Before April or Semi could come to his rescue, he blurted, "Jail."

Semi engaged in a brief coughing fit.

"That a fact," Hack said, darting a severe look at April which she knew from experience meant, *We'll discuss this later, young lady*.

She bestowed fond smiles all around. "Hack, I know it's past your bedtime, so how about if we turn in and get better acquainted in the morning?"

"I second that motion," came a scratchy voice from the shadows down the room by the empty fireplace.

A chair thumped as the woman left it to walk toward them. Dressed in a plaid flannel robe, her arms folded across the shelf of her bosom, she was short and wide, with a pouty mouth, bushy black hair, and eyebrows to match.

"Patsy here has to get up early in the morning," Hack growled. "To catch a bus."

"My last day." Patsy sniffed and continued to look pained.

"Your last day?" April prompted politely.

Patsy nodded, her mouth clamping down on whatever else there was to say.

"Okay. Well. Let's call today a day, then," April said, feeling inane and angry about it. Who the hell was this rude woman anyway? She hadn't been here the last time April visited. The horrible thought that Patsy might be Hack's love interest in his declining years made April blurt out, "Are you related to my grandfather? To me?"

"Oh, God, no," Patsy bleated, reassuring and insulting at the same time. "I hired on to be the housekeeper. Temporarily. You have to put on a show of looking for work, you know, or the unemployment people cut you off."

Semi was nodding, understanding this.

April guessed that her grandfather paid the minimum wage and demanded too much for his money. Patsy probably had a reason for looking as sour as she did.

"Today was her absolutely, positively last day," Hack roared, making everyone except Patsy jump. Then he wheezed three horrible dry chuckles.

"I'll get the bags," Semi said, striding toward the door.

"I'll help," Gayner volunteered, nearly overrunning him.

Without wishing anyone a good night, Hack exited in the opposite direction. As soon as he was out of sight, Patsy swept the kitten off the table with a practiced backhand.

April surveyed the familiar room and began to relax. She'd made many a batch of cookies on that cabinet top, washed many a dish in that double bore sink, toasted many a toe by that fieldstone hearth.

The porters came stamping in with the assorted luggage, breathing hard from the cold and their exertion.

Patsy opened the kitchen closet door that was really the entryway into a steep, narrow stairwell, and they all trooped up, April in the lead. Cold settled on their shoulders and the hint of mothballs brushed their noses. The bare steps creaked and cracked.

At the top, April turned instinctively to the left and her old room.

"Not there. That's mine," Patsy said, pushing past the group to usher them farther down the hall. "Your son can use this bed." She opened the door to the smallest room in the line. "And you two can sleep in here. It's not real dusty," she said, reaching across the hall to unlatch the door of what had been April's mother's bed-sitting room.

Semi raised his eyebrows at April.

She said, "Gayner is a little nervous about sleeping in a strange place, so my husband's going to sleep with him."

"You're kidding." Patsy's mynah-bird voice was as abrasive as a beak on a blackboard.

"Besides," April invented, "I feel a head cold coming on."

One of the house's five toilets flushed, as if editorially commenting on her excuses. Farther along the hall, the bathroom door shuddered open and Hack stepped out.

"Newlyweds that don't want to sleep together," Patsy said in an appeal to him. "Don't that beat all?"

Hack scowled at them, making April stammer, "It isn't that—that we don't *want*—"

"Come on, honey," Semi said, herding her toward the bigger room. "Gayner's a big boy and I'm not afraid of your cold. Good night, all." His hand was warm and firm on the small of her back as he hauled the door shut behind them.

Turning, she stage-whispered, "What's the big idea? We can't sleep—"

"Shh. Your grandfather was beginning to wonder about us. How come you're upset about sharing a room? Surely you'd expected that—"

"What I expected was we'd be given my old room," she snapped. "It has twin beds."

"Well, there's no reason why we can't share this room. We're two levelheaded, self-controlled adults. We can be in close proximity without coming on to each other. I'm not going to bite you."

Ignoring the odd little shiver his last words touched off, April strolled to the four-poster bed and sat down. "You're right. I'll take this and you can have the sofa." She pointed at the latter with her chin.

Brown leather, with wooden arms and a seat that bowed upward, it measured maybe five feet in length. Semi studied the rest of the furniture, obviously searching for an alternative. There was a bureau, two end tables, a bookcase, a writing desk, and a hardwood floor scantily covered by a faded fringed carpet. Two doors on one wall were ajar to disclose a walk-in closet the size of a one-car garage, and a bathroom containing a graceful white tub on bowed legs.

Making up his mind, he wrenched open a suitcase and rummaged for pajamas. "We'll bundle."

"We'll what?"

"Isn't that what they called it when Early American couples courted in the winter? You can wrap up in covers on your side, and I'll wrap up in covers on my side of the bed." He shook out the knit pants he'd been looking for: a yellow-and-black tiger print.

April was too preoccupied to laugh. She thought he ought to at least have the decency to remain fully clothed. "You're going to wear pajamas?"

"Yeah. I'm modest." He carried them into the bathroom and shut the door. A moment later there was the unmistakable snick of the lock engaging.

After a few seconds of contemplating the ceiling, April scrambled off the bed and removed her own pajamas and robe—classically tailored white satin—from her bag. She slipped into the outer hall, intending to use the main bathroom. Frowning at Gayner's closed door, she paused and lightly rapped on it.

Given permission, she inched it open. He was already in bed, covered to his nose, the overhead light on. His khaki duffel bag sat neatly zipped on the only chair. Either he was incredibly tidy, or he was still wearing all *his* clothes, sneakers included.

"You okay, Gayner?"

He nodded.

"Did you find the bathroom all right?"

Another nod.

"Good night, then."

"April?" He swallowed. "Your grandfather doesn't walk in his sleep or anything, does he?"

"No. And don't be afraid of him. He's not as bad as he looks." She stepped close to the bed to give his suspiciously hard foot an encouraging squeeze. "You don't walk in your sleep, do you?"

"Uh-uh." A gleam animated his eyes. "Semi does, though. He walks and talks and does all kinds of stuff in his sleep."

"Oh?"

"Yeah." Gayner, warming to his revelations, hitched up higher on the pillows. "If Semi asks you for matches, don't give 'em to him. And especially don't let him have anything sharp."

When she left him, Gayner was grinning like a game-show host.

Wearing robe and pajamas, teeth brushed and face scrubbed, April opened the bedroom door cautiously, reconnoitering for Semi. He was apparently resigned to sleeping on the floor after all, lying facedown on the none-too-clean carpet.

She stepped over him, robe tail hoisted out of the way, and slung aside the quilt to insert herself in the bed. "I suppose you'll want some cover?" she grumbled.

"Fifty, fifty-one, fifty-two," he said, pushing up with impressive vigor.

The sheets were icy. April performed snow angels, the friction of arms and legs warming her. "Do you sleepwalk, Semi?"

"Sixty, no, sixty-two."

That imp Gayner.

"Sixty-six, not lately, sixty-nine."

She rolled to the side and glared down at him. "You're cheating."

Collapsing on his face, he mumbled, "Nobody but myself."

For a while she watched him breathe. The hairs on the nape of his neck were curly with sweat; the pajama top strained across his back; the pajama pants hugged his surprisingly compact derriere. He might be cheating on his exercises now, but he had obviously done a good job of them in the past.

When he tensed to rise, she whirled over toward the middle of the bed, feeling guilty. "How about snore? Do you snore?" she demanded.

"No, and I don't grind my teeth or wet the bed, either."

He wandered around the room, seeming in search of something. Emerging from the closet, he brandished a piece of curtain rod. April flinched as he thumped it lengthwise on the bed.

"This is our Berlin Wall, our Maginot Line, our Continental Divide." He sat down, warping the mattress, and pointed. "Your side. My side."

"Fine."

Trying to move away from the center of the bed with his weight distorting it was like trying to swim upstream. Putting her back to him in a fetal position, the universal signal of rejection, she anchored herself with a hand on the bed frame and prepared to spend a restless night.

"I forgot to shut off the light," he said, making no move to remedy that. "You realize what time it is? Only ten-forty. We're missing *Taxi* reruns."

There was a pleasurable heat radiating along the ten inches from his body to hers. She longed to stretch her cold feet into his territory.

Instead she scolded, "Would you be still? You're beginning to sound like Gabriel Meldon."

"No, come on. You're not sleepy either. Talk to me," he insisted. "Nobody sleeps at a slumber party. What are you thinking about?"

"I'm thinking I can't believe I'm lying here with a perfect stranger."

Semi rearranged the covers around his legs. "Nobody ever said I was perfect before."

She laughed into the crook of her elbow, thinking she could be very good friends with this man. "When do you have to be back in the city?"

"Let's see. Today's Friday, Christmas is Sunday. Monday morning I need to go in to the office. So I'll take Gayner home Sunday night."

"I'm afraid he's going to get awfully bored around here. Oh!" She twisted around and sat up. "I don't have anything to give him for Christmas."

"That's okay. I do." He patted her knee. "You didn't know he was coming." He withdrew the hand before she could take offense. "What did you get me for Christmas?"

"That wasn't part of the deal." The water spot on

the ceiling she was daydreaming at looked like Florida or— She looked away hastily.

"Your grandfather will expect us to exchange gifts. I got you something."

Interested in spite of herself, she twisted to look at him. He was lying flat, his hands clasped under his head, grinning at the damaged ceiling.

"What did you get me?" she said.

"Nuh-uh. It's a secret."

Flipping onto her stomach, facing away from him, she shut her eyes.

"Okay, you win," he said. "I'll tell you. I thought to myself what I would get for my wife if I were really married. So I bought a saucepan."

Her smile didn't show in her voice. "Yuck. Thanks a million."

They lay with their private thoughts for a time. The windowpane rattled gently in a growing wind. A distant clock struck eleven. Hearing it, April was a little girl again, anticipating walks in the woods, skating on the pond, popping corn in a black screen wire popper in the fireplace, playing solitaire on the kitchen table.

She dozed, and in her dream she heard her parents quarreling. The voices rose, speaking in tongues, unintelligible except for the unmistakable anger they vented. There was the crack of flesh striking flesh. Little April sat up and saw her mother, suddenly an old woman, suddenly a gibbous skeleton.

Sobbing, April woke and burrowed her face into the first warm, hard chest she came across.

Semi's arms wrapped and gently rocked her. "There, there, there, just a bad dream. You're okay." One hand stroked her back, making wonderful paths of tingling heat.

She smiled through her tears, imagining how often he must do this for one of the foster children. "Sorry.

Here I was expecting you to have some disgusting sleep habit, and I'm the one having a dumb nightmare.'' She held herself very still, not wanting to leave the reassurance of his embrace.

"No problem. Actually, I kind of like it.'' He rested his chin on the top of her head.

"You're a nice man.'' Under her cheek, his chest hair felt springy through the thin pajama shirt.

" 'Nice' isn't exactly how I'd like an attractive young woman to think of me. What else have you got?''

"Intelligent? Patient? Stop me if you see something you like. Compassionate?''

"How about just passionate?'' he said and fitted his face against hers in a soft, quiet kiss.

It wasn't her idea of passionate. It was a pleasant, nonthreatening kiss that almost missed her mouth. Friendly. Comforting. She sighed and began to give it back. Semi's mouth moved more purposefully over hers, and something deep inside her turned a slow somersault.

Then something hard jabbed her on the thigh, and she yanked her lips away, glaring at Semi's innocent expression.

"You can keep that to yourself,'' she snarled.

"What?''

"That.'' And she threw aside the covers, prepared to shame him. The curtain-rod boundary rested against her leg.

Semi picked it up between his thumb and forefinger, as if it were something disgusting, and dropped it out his side of the bed. Feeling ridiculous, April got up and snapped off the light switch, releasing blinding blackness. She lay down on the very edge of the mattress and tucked the blankets tight to her body all around.

"Sweet dreams," Semi said softly.

She grunted and shut her eyes, listening to the woodwork creak and Semi breathe.

Morning poured white light through the dusty window. Squinting, momentarily disoriented, Semi tried to identify the warm pressure along his back. Remembering where he was, he peered cautiously over his shoulder at April Parish's rumpled hair and serene face jammed against his backbone. One shapely leg was thrown across his hip; when he explored it with a cautious hand, he discovered the pajama leg hiked up and a long expanse of silky skin exposed.

He shut his eyes and swallowed hard. *Get away from me, Satan.*

Easing out of her oblivious embrace, he planted his feet on the icy floor, which he found as sobering as a cold shower. When he stood up, April moaned and rolled into his space.

Semi felt a pang of regret that this was not a routine morning; that he was not arising while his real wife slept on; that he was, in fact, still an unloved bachelor who must keep his hands to himself.

After watching April for a moment, he gently drew the covers over her shoulder and retreated to the bathroom and his clothes.

Dressed except for the sneakers dangling from his fingers, he let himself into the hall. After peeking in at a snoring Gayner, he followed the scent of bacon downstairs.

The east-facing room was full of unkind sun that highlighted the peeling wallpaper, scuffed woodwork, and stained ceiling. Cabinet tops, chairs, and floor were littered with linens, pans, groceries, magazines, and cats. There were six of the latter in various attitudes of relaxation. Cobwebs and dust motes hung in the air.

Patsy stood at the range top, spatula poised. She was wearing a white, short-sleeved shirt, a pair of baggy blue jeans, and a black expression.

"Good morning," Semi said, hauling out a chair to sit on while he donned his shoes.

If she answered, it was too low to catch.

Boots stomped on the porch, and April's grandfather loomed in the window of the door before it shivered open. Nodding at Semi, he turned to hang his pea jacket on a wall peg and his shotgun on an overhead rack. He came to the table scrubbing his hands together and dropped into a chair.

"Doing some early morning hunting?" Semi asked.

"Not the kind you mean," Hack rasped. "Patsy, I'll have my breakfast now." He put a hand flat on the table and bent over to cough at his knees.

"What do *you* want?" Patsy demanded of Semi.

"Whatever Mr. Jones is having. Whatever's easy." He had a feeling those were two different menus.

Hack unfolded a bandanna handkerchief and bugled his nose. "Whereabouts are you and April Lynn going to live?"

"Her place." Semi nodded and nodded, his eyes fixed on the red-checked tablecloth. "Yep, her place."

"That boy's mother really in jail?"

"Yes. Yes, I guess she is." It was supposed to be best to stick close to the truth when one lied. "I'm not sure, though. We sort of lost track."

"What for?"

"Well, you know how it is. After the divorce we just didn't keep in touch the way we should have."

"No." The old man's voice deepened with irritation. "What was she in jail for?"

Stick close to the truth. Semi thought about Gayner's mom's prostitution. "I guess it was too many parking tickets."

Patsy thumped a plate of undrained bacon, runny eggs, and pale toast in front of each man.

Semi thanked her and added, "When do you have to meet your bus?"

"I don't. It's too cold to walk to the highway. I'll go tomorrow." She slopped two coffee cups beside the plates.

"We could take you in April's car. So you won't miss Christmas Eve with your family," Semi said, expecting to finally win a smile from the woman.

Instead she exited the kitchen, trailing complaints about what-all she had to do and how she'd just have to make the best of being here one more day.

With his mouth full, Hack said, "What's your line, Semi Ruby?"

"Unemployment." Seeing Hack's outraged expression, Semi was quick to add, "I work for an employment office."

Hack grunted. "Good money in that?"

"Nope."

Semi guessed that he wasn't giving a good impression. For April's sake, he ought to make an effort to please the old tyrant. Forcing a smile in place, he said, "I've got a degree in guidance counseling. Someday I'd like to use it in a school setting."

"More money in that?"

Semi sighed. "Nope."

Hack pointed his empty fork at Semi. "Money's not the whole show, you know. You shouldn't think too much on it."

"I thought you were the one who—" Semi took a swallow of coffee to abort the accusation.

"Doing a worthwhile day's work is what counts," Hack continued to expound. "Taking care of your responsibilities. Having children and providing for them."

Semi used the last scrap of toast to wipe up the last

bit of egg yoke before shoveling it into his mouth. It nearly choked him when Hack slapped the table and exclaimed, "There! Where did you learn that?"

"What?" Semi looked down at himself.

"To clean your plate like that. Your grandfather did it, right?"

"Grandpa, yes. And Dad," Semi admitted.

"Exactly my point. Tradition handed down. Generation to generation. Continuity. Genes and environment." He beckoned Semi to lean closer for a confidence. "That's why I wanted April to come to her senses and get married. Even if it's you she had to pick."

"You don't want to be responsible for the Jones line coming to an end," Semi sympathized.

"Damn right! That'd be worse than breaking a chain letter and bringing down a curse." Hack stretched to clap Semi's shoulder in painful camaraderie. "Son, you're better than nobody by a long shot."

"Thank you, sir," Semi said soberly.

The hand tightened on his shoulder, and the old man glowered meaningfully into his eyes. "You make my granddaughter very, very happy."

"I'd like to think so, sir."

They leaned back into their respective chairs and silently contemplated different portions of the high-ceilinged room with its carpet of cats and garage-sale ambiance until April bounded downstairs and fairly skipped into the kitchen.

"Happy Christmas Eve Day!" Wearing an oversized black sweatshirt with "Bengals" on the front, blue jeans faded within an inch of their life, and brown lumberjack boots, she looked seventeen. She gave her grandfather a quick peck on the cheek and patted Semi's arm.

Partly for Hack's benefit, but mostly for his own, Semi trapped her cool fingers and brought them to his mouth. Turning her open palm to his lips, he tenderly kissed that, too. She tasted like soap and smelled like jungle flowers.

Flushing, she disengaged herself from his hold and turned away to assemble her own breakfast of oatmeal and orange juice.

"Your grandfather was just saying how glad he is that we got married," Semi said, putting his arm casually around her chair back while she spooned cereal.

"Now the next thing is," Hack enunciated as if addressing a child with zero attention span, "you give this marriage all you've got. Both of you. You know, April, a divorced man isn't the best risk. He's already failed one woman."

Semi stared at the floor, ashamed of his alleged inadequacies.

Hack droned on. "The both of you are going to have to lean over backwards to make this marriage work."

Brightening, Semi said, "That sounds like fun to me."

Hack ignored him. "I'm going to be bitterly disappointed if you don't stick together."

April kicked Semi under the table before he could make a second remark. "We'll be fine, Hack. I've found myself a wonderful man."

She said it so convincingly, Semi had to remind himself it was just another ivory lie.

Buck (the Chin) Fulton had met Dusty Pressberger in Eden Park, and now they strolled behind the Conservatory, shoulder to massive shoulder like two tanks, forcing anyone else off the path. Neither man was in a good humor, one having recently sworn off smoking and the other having promised his wife he'd give up his girlfriend.

"So where do you think he is?" Buck grumbled. "Skipped the country?"

"Nah. He's close. I can feel it." Dusty tipped back his head and howled, "Cliiint! Where are you?" Then he laughed at the faces of a pair of senior citizens who side-shuffled off the sidewalk into a snowbank to give him plenty of room. "He'll turn up. We'll find him."

Buck sighted past his outstretched arm, his thumb up and forefinger extended, and smacked his lips one time. If he had been shooting his real Combat Commander .45 with the half-foot silencer, the ponytailed jogger bobbing along the horizon would have jogged her last.

Bundled against a temperature the sun had failed to improve very much, April and Semi stepped off the back porch and headed north for a walk in the woods. They linked arms, in case Hack was watching, and staggered through the frozen grass and crusty, days-old snow.

"We ought to wait for Gayner to wake up so he can come with us," April said.

"Rip Van Gayner would rather sleep than walk any day, take my word."

"Well, you were certainly up and at 'em early this morning. What did you and Hack talk about before I came downstairs?"

"He asked about my politics and religion and showed me your naked baby pictures."

"He did not." She laughed, but not with conviction.

A fence and a wooden gate crossed their route. Lifting the baling wire loop from its bent nail hook, April said, "What *are* your politics and religion? In twenty-four words or less."

He fastened the gate behind them before answering. "I vote for clean air and I worship women."

She punched his well-padded arm, enjoying the bantering and the exercise and the Christmas-card scenery. Every breath visible, they marched up a natural ramp into the woods proper. Crows, high in bare branches, criticized them. A beady-eyed squirrel came halfway down a tree trunk to shake his tail at them.

"We'll come back with Gayner this afternoon and cut a Christmas tree," April promised.

"We can't get lost in here, can we?" Semi said, rewrapping his wool scarf against the insistent wind.

"No, Hansel. It's just a little woods. But it's got a creek and a pond. And mayapples in the spring. And hedge apples in the fall. And sometimes deer." The path narrowed and April pranced ahead single file.

"I get the feeling you kind of like this farm."

"I love it," she sang over her shoulder.

He raised his voice against a gust of head wind. "Your grandfather came in this morning with a gun, but he said he wasn't hunting."

"He patrols the property for undesirables."

"Like skunks and groundhogs?"

"Like hunters and government men."

He snorted. "Here I was imagining a frail, bedridden, half-blind coot, and he turns out to be a senior soldier of fortune. You told me he was dying, as I recall."

"I just wanted to be sure you'd help me," she confessed. "*You* aren't what *I* expected either."

"Yeah? How do you mean?"

"Well—I didn't notice your sense of humor at first. In your office. You're a lot easier to be with than I thought you'd be."

"You're trying not to hurt my feelings. I know I don't impress women with my looks or my smooth conversation."

"Oh, don't make me cry. I bet you've had lots of

girlfriends.'' She veered off in a different direction, searching for passage through a bush barricade.

"Friends who were girls, yes. In high school I was too shy, in college I was too busy, and lately I've been too lazy to have a love interest. That's going to change."

Holding back a whip branch for him, she smiled. "You sound sure about that."

"Oh, yeah. I'm looking for one good woman."

Stooping to get past the thorny bush put Semi's face close to hers. He paused, bemused by her warmth radiating out at him, pulling him like a sun luring a sunflower. If he leaned forward a few inches, he could taste the softness of her mouth. He let his eyes narrow suggestively.

"Come on," she said, making his heart jump just before she turned away and he realized she meant "Keep walking."

He buried his nose in the scarf and kept walking. What was he, an adolescent with a crush? Just because he'd made up his mind to find a wife, he couldn't expect the first eligible woman who came along to share his determination to fall in love.

"See?" She interrupted his self-pity.

The creek trickled from right to left across their path, choked by snow and a skin of ice, overgrown by weeds and willows.

"Pretty," he said. It was. He could almost see the "sometimes deer" arching their necks to drink.

"The pond's this way," she said, bearing left.

An insolent twig snagged her knit cap, freeing her hair. Helping her retrieve the cap and stretch it down to her earlobes, Semi successfully battled down an impulse to kiss her smile. Goldang! Was he going to feel this way about any pretty woman who came into his office from now until he found one to marry?

"See?" April repeated a few yards farther on.

The partially frozen pond was a wide spot in the creek, maybe fifteen feet across and twenty feet long. One-way rabbit tracks stitched across the middle.

"It used to be bigger, I think," she said wistfully, taking his arm while they contemplated the present and the past. Her perfume flirted under his nose, an inappropriate, tropical scent.

Semi kicked a rock onto the ice and cringed as it gouged the pristine surface.

"If we keep going this way, we'll hit the road, and then we can walk up the lane," she said, letting go of him and starting off.

Through the woods, across a ditch, onto the tire-tracked road, Semi followed her, mostly staring glumly at his own feet. When this little charade was over and he was back in the rut of his life again, he was definitely going to have to find someone attractive and smart. And *interesting*. Like April.

They topped a little rise, the woods on their left petered out, and Hack's house came into view.

"Oh. My. God." Semi shook his head as if to clear it.

Hack's Tax Shelter was a three-story, white-columned, Greek-revival, palatial estate.

FOUR

"Big place, huh?" April said brightly. "When it was built in 1870 by my great-uncle Abner, there was a family of eleven with six servants living in it."

Semi resumed walking. "How'd he make his fortune?"

"Farming in those days was profitable. Plus he owned a grain mill. And his wife was well endowed."

"Nine children—I'll say she was." Semi reached to take her hand. "In case Hack's watching." With two layers of lined gloves between them, the contact couldn't be called erotic. "That many ancestors and you're the only one left?"

"Horrible, isn't it? Wars and accidents and diseases wiped them out."

The lane was steeper than it had seemed last night. They each followed a tire track, arms stretched between them. Two jet contrails marked the sky with a giant X. The birds back at the woods cawed the same unimaginative note.

"I can appreciate why your grandfather wants you married. So the family genes don't go to waste. Don't you feel kind of obligated?"

"Not me. Babies make me itch. That's not to be confused with itching to make babies."

Grinning, he yanked her arm, dragging her into the deeper snow. She shook her hand free and stooped to pack a snowball. They finished the hike in a running battle, with April reaching the back porch first, but only by the expedient of straight-arming Semi away from it into a lilac bush.

After a disapproving look at their noisy entrance, Patsy turned back to the dishes she was washing. Gayner sat at the table nursing a hot chocolate, his legs wrapped around the chair legs, a blue parka tripling his physique.

"Say, you look ready to roll snowmen," Semi said, unfastening his own snow-splattered jacket.

April stopped him with a hand on his sleeve. "Before you take that off, let's bring in some wood for the fireplace."

They trooped back outside, and she led him to the lean-to south of the porch.

Holding out his arms for her to pile the wood on, Semi said, "Your grandfather's in the doorway of that building over there."

"That's a barn. Where were you raised—in a house?"

"How about doing something for his benefit? Something marital?" He grinned at her expectantly.

"You mean like have a fight?" She gently tipped his chin with one finger, but only to fit a last log under it.

"You've sure got a rotten perspective on marriage," Semi scolded, trudging behind her to the kitchen door. "Most married people don't fight. Very often."

"My role models did," she said, shoving the door open and waiting for a cat to cut in front of her. She showed Semi where to dump the wood, put her two twigs on top, and made a decision. "One more load."

Outside again, Semi nudged her and mumbled out the side of his mouth, "He's still there. Come on, kiss me."

Sighing like a martyr, April turned and wrapped her arms around his neck. "We can do this like stage actors do it."

"How's that?" He rested his hands on her hips, imagining he could feel her body heat through all those layers of clothing.

"You just smush faces together, noses in cheeks. It looks like a real kiss. More sanitary."

His hurt, Jack Benny stare made her giggle.

"I'm not that good an actor," he said, and bent to bring his lips to hers.

April had enjoyed the morning so far—the walk, the dialogue, the snowball fight, the anticipation of showing off the house. But none of these compared with the surprising pleasure Semi's mouth was giving her, the warm sensation of his breath on her cold cheek and the even warmer touch of his lips over hers. As the kiss lengthened and deepened, it thawed a path down her throat, softening her backbone, turning her legs to slush.

It had been a long time since anyone had kissed her like this. Demanding yet tender. As it went on, she felt that *no* one had kissed her quite like this.

She was not simply melting, she was burning. Clinging to Semi, she kissed him with open mouth and, for the moment, open heart.

Then the kitchen door banged, and Gayner clattered across the porch to help with the firewood.

April staggered backward, breaking the embrace. Chilly air replaced Semi's warmth against her skin. His glazed eyes blinked and focused on hers. Straightening his shoulders, he mouthed a silent "Wow."

"Can we build a fort instead of a snowman?"

Gayner said, trying to wrestle a log out of the bottom of the cord.

"Top, top," Semi warned, jiggling the boy's elbow to get his attention. "We can build both. And knock before you come out next time."

Gayner laughed and gave April a sidelong look.

She quickly gathered an armload of wood, her cheeks warm again.

As usual, Ralph Greene's car wouldn't start. He'd been sitting in it all night, wrapped in the down bag he used for hunting. He'd had only two beers so he could appreciate the little joke there—that he was using the bag for a different kind of hunting. He'd listened to talk radio to stay awake, mouthing back at it and working up a temper. Callers could say the dumbest damn things!

Now, at last, what he'd been waiting for was happening. His sister-in-law's car was backing out of the garage. And he couldn't get his own engine to turn the hell over.

Swearing, he watched Nora's Buick glide to the corner and make a left out of sight. He'd catch her next time. There had better *be* a next time.

Meanwhile, Buck and Dusty had found a guy who knew where Clint had gone. This guy, a friend of Buck's from way back—they were distant cousins, in fact—had said he could give them Clint's address. He might need a big favor himself someday. Only thing was, he didn't have the specific information in his possession right that minute. He'd have to get it from this other guy he knew. Who'd be happy to pass it along to Buck and Dusty.

If the price was right.

* * *

Having built a snow fort and a snow robot with a funnel mouth and tuna-can eyes, April, Semi, and Gayner draped their wet outerwear on a portable clothes rack by the now snapping fire and sat down to lunch. Everyone else had hot dogs and potato chips. April fixed herself a BLT without the B.

Patsy dined sitting sidesaddle on the chair, feet poised like a runner awaiting the pistol. Hack chewed in great, grinding bites, elbows planted on the table and eyes fixed on the wall beyond April's left ear. Semi alternated sandwich bites with coffee sips, smiling vaguely at his plate. Even Gayner, who seemed the likely person to fill any awkward pauses with knock-knock jokes, slumped with disinterest.

After several minutes of trying to engage somebody in polite conversation, April hit upon a subject that enlivened the party far more than she'd expected. "After lunch," she told Semi, "I'll show you and Gayner the rest of the house."

"No, you won't," Hack said. He scraped his chair away from the table and crossed one narrow knee over the other. "Not this trip."

"Why not?"

"Too cold."

April laughed. "Not any colder than outside."

"Too cold," Hack repeated stubbornly. "And dangerous."

"What do you mean dangerous?" she scoffed.

"Loose floorboards. Ceiling's about to fall, some places."

"Come on, Hack, we'll be careful. I love this place and I want to show it off."

"It's my house," the old man exclaimed, jutting out his white-stubbled chin.

"Who you going to call—the police?" April mimicked his tone and his expression. They glared across the cluttered table at each other. April wasn't afraid of Hack—she knew he was mostly bark. Still, he could make her extremely uneasy at times.

Hack recrossed his legs and pondered out loud. "Maybe I ought to see your marriage license."

"What?" April snickered, baffled by the sudden change of subject. "We don't have it with us. Do we, Semi?"

Semi shook his head, glad he could verify the truth for a change.

"I can't let a stranger go roaming around the house," Hack said, folding his arms high on his concave chest.

"Sure," Semi agreed. "I understand."

"Well, I don't!" April slapped a palm on the table. "Semi isn't going to write on a wall or swing from a chandelier. He isn't going to steal any of the moldy old furniture."

"It's okay, dear," Semi soothed, covering her hand with his. "I don't have to see the house."

She rounded on him, eyes blazing. "Oh, yes, you do!"

Gayner looked from face to face, forgetting to chew. Patsy grabbed her empty plate and escaped to the sink.

Semi's patting hand clutched April's convulsively as Hack lunged forward and stared him in the eyes. "You swear you're only here because you love my granddaughter?"

Semi swallowed. "I swear I'm only here—because I—because of her."

Gayner's saucer eyes glowed with admiration for these weasel words.

April found herself holding her breath and was immediately angry again. This wasn't life and death, this was just her pulling her grandfather's leg and him being his usual exasperating self. "Hack—"

"Stubborn," he said, shaking his forefinger at her.

"You got to learn to think of someone else once in a while. Learn compromise."

"Right," she agreed. "I just didn't inherit your knack for diplomacy."

An odd expression flitted across her grandfather's face. Had it been on anyone else, she'd have thought it was amusement.

"Do whatever the hell you want," Hack said, twisting off his chair and marching upstairs.

"Whew, what was that all about?" Gayner breathed.

"He can be such a pill," April said to Semi. "Insulting you like that." She slid her hand out from under his and used it to resume eating.

"Maybe it isn't me personally he's worried about."

"What do you mean?"

"Well, maybe—" Semi sent an uncomfortable glance toward Patsy, who was slamming dirty dishes into a precarious stack. "Maybe there's something in the house he doesn't want just anyone to see."

April stared dumbly. "What?"

He shrugged. "A private arsenal?"

"No." Her tone settled it. "He thinks that you married me for my money and you can hardly wait to count it."

"This is the dining room," April said, a reluctant Semi and an intrigued Gayner in tow.

It was a long empty room immediately behind the kitchen. Their shoes echoed on the wooden floor as they crossed to the double doors at the opposite end. April twisted the knob without success.

"Locked?" Semi said cheerfully. "That's okay. Let's play Monopoly instead."

"We'll go through on the second floor." She brushed past him to lead them to the kitchen stairwell.

Scampering ahead up the steps, Gayner speculated loudly on the possibility of ghosts. He stopped abruptly, making April teeter dangerously on the top step. Semi's hand on her hip was meant to steady her, not, as it turned out, to increase her feeling of precariousness.

"Maybe that's why your grandpa doesn't want you messing around the house," Gayner was saying. "Maybe there's a coffin with Dracula—"

"Don't get your hopes up, Gayner." She shoved him out onto the landing and lightly swatted Semi's hand away. "Or yours either."

As they paced the hall past mostly closed bedroom doors, April tipped her head at one. "That's Hack's room."

"Didn't he say it would be cold in the unused part of the house?" Semi asked.

"Oh, yeah. We'd better put on coats."

"I'll get 'em," Gayner volunteered, already racing back in the direction they'd come.

They waited for him where the hall was barred by a massive wooden door. April slowly turned the knob, more than half expecting this door to be locked as well. It swung away, creaking an ominous welcome. She and Semi peered across the threshold at another dim, door-lined hall.

Scrubbing cool air off her arms, April twisted around to smile at her companion. "How are you holding up so far, Mr. Ruby? Is the job as bad or worse than you expected?"

He studied her gravely before answering. "I like my boss. A lot." He reached out to trap her hand and gently tugged her closer.

"Get smart with me, mister, and you're fired. Out of here," she warned.

"No, listen, I just want—"

"I know what you want—"

Their little tussle ended with his stronger arms inevitably drawing her into kissing range. She found herself willingly tipping her face to improve his aim. The kiss felt so good—too good.

And she had no intention of letting this man—or any other man—get under her skin.

Defensively she pulled back and snapped, "Now listen—"

"Come on, April," he murmured. "It's just a kiss. It isn't anything personal."

She gasped for air, intending to flay his ears with a cutting reply, but his mouth dropped over hers again, and she changed her mind. What could be wrong, after all, about something as sweet and gentle as this? As warm and pleasant as this? As exciting and knee-weakening as this?

She thought her heart was audibly pounding till she realized Gayner had rejoined them and was ostentatiously knocking on the wall. As they moved apart, he pushed coats at them and stepped eagerly through the gaping door.

"Okay if I look in here?" he asked, his hand on the first bedroom door.

"Sure." She jammed her hands in the coat pockets, finding crumbs of unmelted snow.

It was a large, dusty room, full of large, dusty furniture. Gayner opened the closet door and leaped back when a stack of musty books collapsed through it.

He held up a hand for silence. "Did you hear that?"

"No, what?" April said, expecting a joke.

"A baby crying. No, really," Gayner insisted. "Listen."

Everyone stood still for half a minute, ears straining.

"One of the cats," April said.

Semi threw an arm around the boy to pull him to the hallway. "You're going to be too wound up tonight to sleep."

"Hey, yeah, that's when we should explore," Gayner said. "At night. With candles."

As they strolled from room to room, finding some empty, some cluttered with Victorian furniture, April was remembering the fun she'd had as a little girl, exploring and pretending.

They came to the front of the house, where an intersecting hall stretched in both directions and a sweep of steps led down to the main floor.

"Man, this house don't quit," Gayner marveled.

"It was like a palace in a fairy tale to me when I was a child." April put one hand on the graceful mahogany banister and stared down at the entryway's marble floor. She sniffed.

Semi put a comforting hand on her shoulder, embarrassed by her emotion, and then jumped when she rounded on him to ask, "Do you smell cigarette smoke?"

He sniffed with her this time. Gayner threw back his head and turned in every direction, doing more than his share of noisy inhaling.

"Maybe the baby's picked up the filthy habit early," Semi said.

"So you smell it?"

"No."

Gayner added his regretful headshake to the vote. "Let's go down here," he said, putting the suggestion into action, hippity-hopping down the steps.

Semi stretched a tentative arm around April's waist as they started down the broad staircase. When she didn't snarl at him, he tugged her closer, distracting her with a casual observation: "I bet you came down this the night of your senior prom to meet your date. He was a skinny kid in a rented tux, and you were a vision in a blue strapless formal. Wrist corsage, right?"

April blinked at the sudden sting of tears. She'd spent prom night hiding out in her room, sketching self-portraits with imaginary young men. All of them were tall, of course, and all bent toward her with encouraging, cherishing smiles. Not one looked capable of raising his voice to her, let alone his hand.

"April?" Semi's voice was as low and full of concern as she could have longed for, all those years ago.

"Oh, Semi," she murmured mournfully. "I wish I'd known you then. Before it got too late."

He stopped her short of the next step, his arms hard around her. "Hey, don't say 'too late.' We're just getting started here, you and me. We can work anything out. Talk to me."

She rested her nose in the hollow of his neck, fighting tears, hating this helpless weakness. It would be such a relief to let go, to let Semi into her life. But her mother had trusted a charming, desirable man like this, and he'd betrayed her with mental and physical abuse.

April's paralyzing fear was that she would fall for a man like dear old Dad.

Shaking her hair free of Semi's gently stroking hand, April willed ice into her eyes and voice. "Thank you, Semi, but I'm fine. Silly of me to grieve over not having had a date for the prom after all these years."

"Hey, maybe you didn't miss much anyway," he said in an attempt to soothe her. "I went to my senior prom and spent two hundred bucks on clothes, food, and a girl who didn't give me anything in return except a lousy good-night kiss and mono for the rest of the school year."

"Oh, Semi," she said again, somewhere between a laugh and a sob. Patting his cheek, she let him see the ice had melted before she turned to finish their descent.

Gayner waved at them to hurry up.

"On your left, gentlemen," April droned like a tour guide, "are, in railroad-car progression, the library, the music room, and a sun porch/conservatory. If you turn right, the rooms are parlor, ballroom, and second kitchen. In front of you is the front door and the veranda. Under the stairs and straight back, several small rooms lead to the dining room we tried to come through earlier.''

"What kind of ball?" Gayner asked, galloping off without waiting for an answer.

"He thinks a ballroom is a basketball court," Semi explained, strolling in the same direction. "These rooms don't seem very cold."

April frowned. He was right. The temperature, though not warm, wasn't what you'd expect in an empty house in December. She was surprised Hack was willing to pay the fuel bill to keep this part of the building livable.

They walked into the parlor and April frowned again. It looked like a stage set for a turn-of-the-century melodrama: dark velvet chairs, heavy wood tables, a black upright piano, ornately framed watercolors, tasseled and brocaded drapes. There were even yellowing antimacassars and doilies sprinkled about the furniture. The fireplace held three logs ready for a match. There wasn't more than one layer of dust over everything.

Hack must be using this room. But why?

She followed Semi into the ballroom, where Gayner, obviously disappointed by the vast empty space, was trying unsuccessfully to slide on the gritty floorboards. Semi's hand grasped her arm, drawing her to a halt. He pointed at the floor, where a path of footprints led through the dust to the second kitchen's closed door.

"Should those be there?" he said.

"Listen," Gayner piped up. "Spooky music."

Holding her breath, April heard the unmistakable phrasing of Frank Sinatra's "I've Got You Under My Skin."

Puzzled, she shook off Semi's hand and marched forward. If she'd thought of intruders, she would have been more angry than afraid. As it was, her impression that Hack must be using this kitchen, too, struck her as odd but not alarming.

Semi and Gayner were at her elbows when she pushed open the heavy door and peered in. All three of them froze as four faces peered back.

There were two men standing by the sink. The smaller, fair-haired one made an unmistakably threatening gesture of darting his hand beneath his jacketed armpit. The stocky, dark man did a quick bob that might have been a halfhearted attempt to duck under nonexistent cover.

The other two people were a pale young woman and the moon-faced baby she was bottle-feeding at the table, which was cluttered with the remains of the adults' meal. The mother jerked so hard at seeing the unexpected company that the nipple wrenched free, and a wail of complaint sirened the scene.

In unison, April and the man with his hand inside his jacket said, "Who are you?"

April drew herself up to her full height. "I'm the granddaughter of the owner of this house. What are you doing here?"

"Who's that with you? Come in where I can see you, mister."

Semi, moving slowly, his hands out in front to show his harmlessness, said, "I'm the grandson-in-law. Does Hack know you're here?"

Taking his hand, which was empty, out of his jacket, the man circled warily to their side of the room and, at arm's length, patted Semi's clothes before leaning past April to reconnoiter the ballroom. Gayner shrank away from his brief, speculative glare.

"Sorry," the stranger said, retreating and shrugging

to relax his shoulders. "Have to be careful of burglars, the place being full of antiques and all."

Antiques, April was certain, were the least of this man's worries.

The baby's bottle was back in position, and his screams were replaced by the tinkle of easy-listening radio music. The mother's tense expression softened into a tentative smile at April. Stumbling from the sink to a chair beside the table, the swarthy man sagged into it and fumbled a pack of cigarettes out of his shirt pocket.

The first man said, "Hack must not have mentioned he's renting out rooms to us. I'm Ivan Como. That's Clint Ajax. This is Sherry Greene, and her Casey."

Clint, lighting the cigarette with palsied fingers, remarked in a surprisingly high voice, "You'd think Hack would have said something about relatives snooping around."

"You'd think he would have said something about us to the relatives." Ivan produced a weak imitation of a smile.

"That's Hack for you," April said. "He'd have loved to have seen us all a minute ago." She sauntered to the table and sat down. "What do you do for a living, Mr. Como?" She looked pointedly at the bulge under his jacket.

"I'm a freelance writer. Need lots of peace and quiet." He folded his arms and rocked on his heels, plainly daring her to call him a liar.

"And you, Mr. Ajax?" she asked like a hostess at a party.

He puffed smoke, rolling panicky eyes. "I'm a freelance writer," he finally decided.

"And you, Ms. Greene?" April's voice dripped sweetness. "What is it you write?"

"Nothing," Sherry said with an air of regret. "I used to write song lyrics, though, just for the fun of it."

"So if you aren't in need of peace and quiet to write, what are you doing here?" April smiled and waited.

"I'm recovering from an accident," Sherry said, and she shook back her fine, straight hair, tilting her face to the overhead light. The skin around her eyes was tinged with green, the last stage of a bad bruise.

"Oh, I'm sorry," April said truthfully. The infant's serene gaze inspected her over the bottle. "Is the baby all right?"

"He's fine." His mother swayed him gently, admiring him. She was wearing a too-big army jacket that emphasized the thinness of her wrists and ringless fingers.

"How long have you been here?" April asked, sympathy overriding antagonism. "Is it warm enough for a baby?"

"About two months. He's four months now. I keep him bundled up good." She raised her head to smile at Gayner. "Is this your boy?"

"Yes. Gayner." April snared him with one hand and pulled him, feet dragging, into the circle of her arms. She tried to look maternally proud.

"I didn't see your car." Semi addressed Ivan, who had moved back to lounge against the refrigerator.

"It's in the barn."

"Well, so, Mr. Ajax"—April launched a fresh assault—"what exactly do you write? Poetry?"

Caught in the act of stabbing out the cigarette, he jerked it to his mouth instead, his eyes wide with the effort of sucking on an extinct fire.

"We're collaborating on a biography," Ivan interceded, smooth as a snake.

"Whose?"

"Fella name of Augie Swillman. Mass murderer in Akron. All his victims were brown-haired, very tall, slender, attractive women. Gutted them with a posthole digger." His grin showed every tooth.

"Fascinating," April said, jumping as Semi's hand dropped onto her shoulder.

"We better go, honey."

Gayner scrambled out of her embrace, not needing to be told twice. He rebounded off the doorframe and was gone.

"What do *you* do for a living, and I didn't catch your name?" Ivan stared at Semi.

"Semi Ruby. I find jobs for honest citizens." He put a little extra emphasis on "honest." Stretching across April, he offered his hand to Ivan, who didn't hesitate more than five seconds before clasping it.

"And I'm April," she said to Sherry.

The girl hooked her hair behind one ear, revealing another chartreuse bruise along her neck. "Nice to meet you." She beamed at everyone, as if all differences had been settled. "You have a nice-looking son." Her eyes lingered on Semi. "And husband."

"Let's go," April said, almost chinning Semi as she leaped to her feet. "See you." She linked arms with her nice-looking husband and pointed him through the door. "We have to go cut a Christmas tree, darling. I'll show you the rest of the house some other day," she bellowed into his ear as they crossed the echoing ballroom.

As soon as they were in the parlor, she shook free of him and tiptoed fast toward the front entry, hissing over her shoulder, "Shh, hurry. This way." And she turned under the stairs toward the rear of the house, where they hadn't yet explored.

"April—"

"They must be sleeping in the little rooms between here and the dining room. There's a sewing room and a den and a playroom. Big enough for beds."

"April, you aren't going to snoop—"

"Good heavens, no. I'm just going to look."

Their entourage now included Gayner, who'd been waiting for them beside the stairway, shifting from foot to anxious foot. "You think they're drug dealers?" he asked, checking over his shoulder at frequent intervals.

"I don't know, but they're up to something." April paused by the first closed door in the dim hall under the stairs.

She eased the knob around and gently pushed. Semi helped Gayner look nervously back the way they'd come.

The room, all dark wood and empty bookshelves, had been built as a den. Now it contained one twin-sized brass bed, one baby's crib, and five boxes of disposable diapers.

"Aha," Semi breathed at her ear. "They're diaper smugglers."

She drew the door shut as quietly as she'd opened it and moved on to the next room. This one was even smaller than the first, but the renters had managed to get a double bed into it. The smell of stale tobacco and the size of the underwear littering the floor identified Clint's quarters.

"I don't like this," Semi said to Gayner. "Do you like this?"

Gayner shrugged. "Kind of."

The third room April remembered as open and bright, with yellow wallpaper and many windows. But when she eased the door wide, it was like entering a theater in mid-movie—dark and vaguely threatening. She fumbled along the wall to find the overhead light switch. This room, like the other two, was almost filled by a bed.

The odd thing was, every window was completely covered by what looked like bed sheets nailed to the frames.

Semi's clutching hand missed April's arm as she strode into the room. She leaned over to examine a spill of books on the neatly made bed: *Lock Picking Simplified, Making a Gun in Your Home Workshop, How to Get a New ID*, and four books with "counterfeit" in the titles.

"Just look at this." April struggled to keep her voice down in spite of her outrage. She picked up a banded bundle of hundred-dollar bills from a dresser top and rippled them at the worried faces in the doorway. "He's using my home to counterfeit money." She slapped the bills back where she had found them.

"Come on, April," Semi demanded. "Out. Now."

Still muttering to herself, she let him lead her into the hall to the door they couldn't open from the other side an hour earlier.

Gayner spun on one toe while he waited for Semi to use the key that was in the lock. "You gonna call the cops?"

"Yes," April said, and "No," Semi said. They gave each other offended looks as the door creaked aside to let them into the dining room.

"You're going to discuss it with your grandfather first," Semi told her.

"Oh. Naturally," she conceded.

"I hesitate to mention it—" He did hesitate. "The illegal activities going on under Hack's roof may not come as a surprise to him."

"Oh," she said again.

She became aware of Semi's fingers laced with hers. It reminded her of her first day of school, when her mother's reassuring grip had been horrible to relinquish.

Tightening the hold, she clumped the last lap of their circuitous route to the welcome warmth of the kitchen. Hack sat by the snapping fire, polishing pieces of a shotgun with a ragged tea towel.

FIVE

"Grandfather! You're just the man I wanted to see," April said with false enthusiasm. She dragged Semi to the other chair flanking the hearth, pushed him down into it, and perched on his knee. Opening her coat, she said, "You didn't tell me you had boarders."

"Nope. You have to admit, though, I did my damnedest to warn you not to go prowling around the house." Hack didn't look up, but he smiled at his work.

She took a bolstering breath, glancing around the familiar, shabby room. Gayner had squatted strategically near the back door and was pretending fascination with a rock doorstop.

"Ivan Como is counterfeiting money," April said, watching Hack's face for a reaction and getting none. "He's studying stuff like how to build a machine gun and how to change his identity."

"That so?" Hack exhaled on whatever he was polishing and rubbed with fresh vigor.

"He's wearing a gun in a shoulder holster," April practically wailed, beginning to feel like a tattletale being snubbed by her teacher. "Hack, he's dangerous!"

Resting his hands on his knees, Hack looked her in the eye. "I believe you're right. He's dangerous." Picking up a different gun part to clean, he added, "I like him."

"Hack!"

"Sir, if he's breaking the law, you could be considered an accessory," Semi said, his breath stirring April's hair.

Hack's amusement showed as a few seconds' twitch of his mouth.

Completely exasperated, April threw up her hands. "Hack, he could kill us all in our beds!"

"April Lynn, you have my written guarantee that if we're all killed in our beds, it won't be Ivan Como who did it."

"That's supposed to make me feel better? Are you saying Clint Ajax is the hit man in the gang? Or maybe Mama Sherry? Would you please give me a straight answer about something just *once*?"

"Bet you didn't know what a nervous Nellie you'd married there, Mr. Ruby," Hack began to reassemble the shotgun with sure, sharp motions.

April bobbed to her feet. "I'm calling the police."

"Set," Hack said, pointing a gnarled forefinger at Semi's lap. When she'd unwillingly complied, her grandfather returned his attention to the shotgun, speaking as if to it. "You are not to call in any authorities, understand? Ivan Como and the rest of those people are not out to harm us. You have to take my word for it. If you don't, you'll have to pack up and git."

Semi's hard, warm arms tightened warningly. "It's okay," he said against her backbone. "I'm sure Hack knows what he's doing. Come on, let's go cut a Christmas tree." He stood slowly, setting her on her feet, keeping one supportive arm around her shoulders.

Hack grumbled, "I do know what I'm doing, which is more than I can say for you, April Lynn."

She flapped her hands, defeated.

Gayner ripped open the back door for them and cantered into the yard. "We need a chain saw. You got a chain saw? Can we pick a ten-foot tree? You got that many decorations? You got *any* decorations?"

"There's probably an ax in the barn," April said, allowing Semi to button her coat, her mind rerunning the scene with Hack.

They trudged after the capering boy, snow crackling underfoot. One orange tiger cat scampered around them, her tail like a bottlebrush, on an errand of her own to the barn. The sun grazed the southern horizon.

April shivered and bumped closer to Semi. "The old fool," she muttered.

"I can check on whether Como's wanted by the police when I'm back in Dayton." He squeezed her against him a couple of times. "You want to go home with me?"

"Yes, but someone needs to keep an eye on Hack, make sure he doesn't get into real trouble. Besides, I'm not going to let a little band of riffraff run me off my own place. I came to have a pleasant Christmas vacation, and, by God, I'm going to have a pleasant Christmas vacation—"

"If it kills you," Semi finished for her. He paraphrased her earlier remark. "The young fool."

"You think so?" She was worried.

"I think you'll be just fine. Any friend of Hack's has got to be a sweetheart. But, April"—he searched for the right words—"how likely is it that your grandfather invited those people because they are a gang and he's—ahhh—"

"The gang leader? Oh, I'd say chances are not more than—"

Her shoulders slumped in a gesture of despair. "Fifty-fifty." She kicked out at a lump of snow, shattering it into cold powder. "He's never done anything really criminal that I know of, but he's always been a rebel."

They stopped in the open doorway of the barn, and Semi made her look at him. "I'll worry about you when I leave. And I'm going to miss you." Before her surprise could translate into a fitting response, he turned away. "Whoops, I'll carry that," he said to Gayner, who'd already located the ax and was swinging it like a golf club.

All three of them paused momentarily to study Ivan Como's car parked in the dusty center of the mostly empty barn. Instead of the sleek black limousine April had envisioned, it was a white compact car a lot like hers.

They trooped into the woods far enough to find a graceful Douglas fir that Gayner complained about being too small the entire ten minutes it took for Semi to chop it down.

"Dull ax," April said, tactfully ignoring the splintery evidence of his poor aim.

Dragging their prize back to the house, they sang Christmas carols.

Supper was Patsy's version of smorgasbord. She emptied the refrigerator of leftovers, heated everything to the point of combustion, and thumped down a quart bottle of catsup for a centerpiece. While the rest ate, April put the finishing touches on the ribboned and tinseled tree, which they had erected a safe twelve feet from the fireplace.

Squinting critically at it, she crossed to stand behind Semi and rested her arms on his shoulders. Funny, how natural that felt to her; how comfortable she was with him. Too bad being married wasn't as good as this.

Mischievously, she kissed the back of his neck while she reached for his plate to steal a scrap of ham. Too bad friendship couldn't last past the wedding vows.

He pinched up another bite of meat and offered it over his head in the direction of her mouth. Gayner laughed when she missed and lost it in Semi's hair. Patsy snorted disapproval. Hack chewed with total absorption, as if he were alone.

"It's Christmas Eve," April said. "Let's open our presents."

"Christmas morning is when you open presents," Semi declared. "Right, Patsy? Right, Gayner?"

Patsy ignored him; and Gayner, his eyes shining, voted to do it April's way.

It was an odd, make-do exchange among people who'd been strangers two days before. April had found a crisp five-dollar bill in her wallet for Gayner, and an unused perfume among her cosmetics for Patsy. Hack had dredged up a brittle-paged coloring book and crayons that Gayner outdid himself at being thrilled to receive. April gave Hack a thick, gray fisherman's sweater, and Semi a briefcase. Contrary to what he'd told her, Semi's gift to her was a delicate gold chain bracelet.

She saw Hack slip Patsy an envelope. April hoped it was a nice bonus and not a solitary Christmas card. Hack handed Semi a brown paper bag.

"Gosh, I was hoping for a cat," Semi joked, rustling the top open. He peeped in, gave April an enigmatic blink, and carefully poured the contents into his hand. They were six bullets and one mean-looking revolver.

"Sir, this is nice of you," Semi struggled to say. "But I don't know anything about firearms. I don't really need—something this—final. Fine. Something this fine."

"Maybe you haven't needed it up to now," Hack

said. "Never know when you might. April can show you how to use it. I gave her one about like it for her twentieth birthday."

Semi gave her a befuddled look. She nodded reassuringly at him, advising, "Smile, pardner."

Hack produced a second brown sack and held it out to April. Copying Semi, she peeked inside before inserting her hand to reverently withdraw the pearl-and-diamond confection.

"Grandmother's brooch," she breathed, extending her palm for everyone to ooo. "Oh, Hack, you gave it to her for her wedding dress. This is an honor you'll never—" She hid her face by bowing it to pin the brooch to her black sweatshirt, with Semi's help.

Rising, Hack hitched up his trousers and stalked out of the room, precluding any hugs or attempted kisses.

Patsy yawned and stretched extravagantly before she, too, stood up and crossed to the stairs.

"See you tomorrow," April called after her.

"Maybe. Depends on if you get up before I leave. It's my last day, you know."

"Oh, yes. Of course, you want to be with your family on Christmas," April said.

"What family? The few I got are even crazier than yours. I stay way away from them." Patsy stamped up the steps.

Laughing, Semi draped an arm over April's shoulders. Gazing around the shadowy room, she felt the old familiar letdown of no more Christmas gifts to unwrap. Gayner was using the table as a racetrack for the handful of miniature cars that Semi had given him. The competition seemed to have more than its share of horrendous accidents.

Semi's quiet voice tickled her ear. "I'll never forget this Christmas Eve with you, April Lynn Parish."

She leaned companionably into him. "That's quite a

compliment. I bet you've had lots of memorable Christmases with your family and all the children who've lived with you."

"You'll have to spend next Christmas with us," he said. "You'd love it."

"Maybe." She looked down the long, mental corridor to her youth. "I'm not sure I'd enjoy a bunch of kids around. My holidays were always just the three of us. Quiet."

"You'd love it," he repeated confidently.

Gayner's automobile sound effects segued into a fit of yawning.

"Better hit the mattress, kiddo," Semi told him. "How about you, pretty lady? Ready to go to bed?"

April turned her face into his collarbone and moaned. It had been such a busy, emotional day. Bed sounded wonderful. But bed with Semi in it was going to be one more grueling test of her nerves.

Dusty turned his back to the party and hunched over the receiver, a forefinger in his free ear. "Say it again?"

Buck complied with an impatient growl. "The guy who claimed he could help us find Clint? Now he says he can't."

"What? He wants more money?"

"Naw, I don't think he knows. He was just running off at the mouth after too many drinks. I think we—"

Something crashed in the kitchen, and the crowd cheered. Dusty cringed. If this was Christmas Eve, what would his wife's family do to New Year's? Holding the mouthpiece against his barrel chest, he shouted a warning over his shoulder, every other word blue. His voice sank into the uproar without a trace.

When he put the phone to his ear again, Buck was saying, ". . . few days. What do you think, Dus?"

What Dus thought was that he'd take this new frustration out on the next person who laughed too loud.

"Merry Christmas," he said into the receiver.

April took a long, hot bath, hoping Semi would be asleep when she returned.

But he lay with his hands clasped behind his head, staring at the ceiling, blanketed below the waist, his wide, curly-haired chest bare to the chilly room. "Know what I'd like right now?"

Afraid to guess, and also afraid to join him in bed, she busily folded and unfolded clothes.

He rolled up on one elbow. "Can you get pizza delivered out here?"

"You didn't get enough ham jerky?"

He laughed. "Patsy did overcook it a tad. There was a pizza here last night."

"Right. And a box in the trash that told how to thaw and bake it. You'll have to brave it out till you get back to the city." Her ankles were getting cold, but Semi certainly didn't look sleepy, so she rearranged the clutter of cosmetics on the dresser. "Speaking of being brave, maybe you should sleep with Gayner tonight."

"He said he wasn't scared."

"Well, *I* am. I mean I'm worried. About those people. So I'd think Gayner would be, too."

"Gayner likes to be scared. Except by his mother and her sleazy friends." He watched April, frowning. "Can't whatever you're doing wait till morning?"

She crumpled the paper bag that had held the brooch and scanned the area for the other brown bag. "What did you do with the revolver?"

"Hid it in the closet where Gayner won't find it."

"Good idea. But then again—" she stopped fidgeting, feeling like a windup toy that had finally run down. "Maybe you ought to carry it with you. Like the rest of the hombres around here."

"No, thanks. I don't want to hurt anyone, especially myself."

"Oh. So." She turned around and looked him in the eye. "Have you got any pants on?"

First he laughed, then he leered, and then he whipped off the blanket, revealing the tiger-print pajama bottoms in all their gaudy glory. "Is that why you've been hovering out of reach like a vulture waiting for the last gasp?"

It irritated her enough to bat the light switch and march to bed. Stabbing both feet into the cocoon of covers, she inadvertently touched his foot and jerked away as if she'd been burned. Burrowing into her pillow, her back to him, she faked a noisy yawn and said good night.

There were perhaps two minutes of absolute silence before he said, "I could sure use some safe sex with a consenting adult about now."

"I knew it!" She sat up, scattering bedding. "I knew you were going to pester me like this."

"Pester? What did I do?"

"Harass. It's against the law to sexually harass someone you work for."

"You've got it backward or sideways or something," he said, struggling to sit up, too. "You're my boss, so you can't make advances to me, which means that I have to do it if it's going to get done."

She put her face into her updrawn knees, determined not to reward him with a laugh. "Semi, just go to sleep, would you?"

The bed jiggled as he settled down. She hugged her legs, remembering how nice his kisses had felt. Sleet began to hiss against the windows.

Semi's words were muffled by the blankets. "What do

you want this huge house for if you aren't going to have a husband and children?''

"I beg your pardon?''

"I guess you'd be set for life if you could sell it at the right time, huh? The acreage alone must be worth millions.''

Horrified at the thought, she sputtered, "Sell? Sell? This wonderful place?'' Biting her tongue, she started over more calmly. "I don't think it's any of your—''

"You know what would be great? This layout would make a terrific children's home.'' He was getting louder as he warmed to the notion. "Kids would love it out here. Well, you know that, because you did.''

"It isn't going to be a children's home. I'm not going to have a dozen kids of my own. I didn't hire you to help me wheedle my grandfather into leaving me the farm. I hired you to help me make him happy.'' She accented the last words with a shove to his chest, forgetting she was trying not to touch him.

"Happy. Right. You want him happy with you so he won't be tempted to leave the estate to a bunch of cats.''

"Even if he was furious with me, he wouldn't do anything as dumb as that!'' She grabbed her pillow and swatted him.

"What could be dumber than leaving a fifty-room palace to an old-maid recluse?''

"Arrrg!'' She fell on top of him, her hands on his throat.

And froze as his arms came around her.

He was gurgling with laughter, trying to be quiet. "Help, wait a minute. Let me get my new gun.''

She rested her face on his musky chest, wide-eyed in the dark. "You see? You see how we fight?''

"You call this a fight?'' His chuckle bumped her up and down. "I'm too chicken to fight. That wasn't a fight.'' One of his hands drifted onto her hair and began to stroke it. "Are you angry with me?"

"No." She was angry with herself. For enjoying the comfort of his caress. Worse, she had enjoyed the excitement of their scuffle. She squeezed her eyes shut to discourage the tears she felt welling from the thought: *Dad would be real proud of me*.

To drown out the inner voice, she said out loud, "I know it's selfish, Semi, but I love this estate. I want to come live here and paint. I'd do it now, but Grandfather doesn't like the idea. He's selfish, too, you see." Her laugh was rueful. "What's wrong with making *him* happy so he'll make *me* happy?"

Semi didn't answer, but his thumping heart relaxed her like a lullaby.

He, on the other hand, was not feeling relaxed at all. While his fingers toyed with April's hair, what he really wanted to do was drag her face up to his and kiss her senseless. All the time he'd wasted during the past twenty years—all the lovemaking he'd missed—weighed on him now. This fine woman who felt so great in his arms was definitely his proverbial bird in the hand.

Clearing his throat, he said, "I'd really like to kiss you."

"No. Please. It would only complicate things."

"I *like* complications," he said, tensing to lift her into position.

"Please," she breathed, and then added the words that would assure his good behavior. "I trust you like I've never trusted any man. Just hold me for a while."

Inwardly groaning, he settled his arms lightly across her back. *There's a hell of a lot more to love than sex*, he lectured himself.

"You really never fight?" Her drowsy voice floated upward.

"I'm pretty easy to get along with." He could feel clammy sweat evaporating on his forehead.

"You are," she agreed. "I think I could . . ."

For a while the room's only sound was sleet on glass. Semi prompted tenderly, "You could what?"

For several more moments there was only sleet, and then he heard the disappointing but unmistakable rhythm of her gentle snoring.

"Damn," he whispered and carefully pulled the blankets over her shoulders.

April opened her eyes to a room full of sunlight and Semi staring at her. She had one arm across his neck and one leg straddling his stomach.

"Sorry," she said, hastily backing into her own side of the bed.

"I'm not. What's your hurry?" he complained as she rolled out of bed.

"Polite people don't ask such questions." She sorted out her robe and put it on. "Anyway, it's late. Nine-ten."

"Late for what? You have a plane to catch?"

"If I don't eat breakfast now, I won't be hungry in time for lunch." She tightened the belt in a complicated knot she knew she'd regret later.

"You don't eat breakfast or lunch. I've never seen you sit down and eat a meal containing all the food groups." He peeled back the covers and swung his feet into slippers.

"I'd have eaten a hearty lunch the first day I met you if you hadn't been too cheap to take me out."

"I didn't know you. Why risk an expensive meal on a possibly impossible female?"

"Nothing ventured, nothing gained, buster."

"You're right," he said, grabbing her around the

waist and bestowing the kiss he'd been dreaming about all night.

For the first ten seconds of the kiss, April wriggled and murmured her outrage. For the next ten seconds, she stood unresisting and unresponsive in the circle of his arms. For all the many seconds after that, she relaxed and enjoyed the roller coaster her stomach was riding.

Knees buckling, they sank to the edge of the bed. When Semi began to push her backward toward the mattress, she jerked away and staggered to her feet.

"My God, Semi!" Hugging herself, she backed away from his reach. "I don't know how I could let you tempt me like this. Quit!" She sidestepped again and slapped at his persistent hand.

"Don't be embarassed. It's okay to have feelings like this."

"Just leave me alone," she insisted, rushing into the bathroom and slamming the door.

Leaning on the other side, she fanned her hot face with one hand and silently scolded herself for letting her resolve slip. Semi might be desirable—*very* desirable—but he wasn't *her* desire.

Breathing normally again, she crossed to the tub and turned on the cold water.

In Cincinnati, slouched low in his derelict Chevy, Ralph Greene watched Sherry's sister load red-and-gold packages with silver bows into the trunk of her car. He tapped the steering wheel and whistled soft, random notes. He'd started up his car as soon as he saw her come out. Ol' Nora was about to show him where his wife had gone.

April and Semi went downstairs together and found Gayner, Hack, and a mob of cats in the late stages of breakfast. Good-mornings were passed around, and April went to the refrigerator to search out orange juice.

"Patsy leave yet?"

"Nope." Hack swung a used tea bag into his cup for a refill.

"Maybe I could give her a lift when I start back to Dayton," Semi offered.

Hack half rose to whisk the tea kettle off the stove and slop boiling water into his cup. "Your new wife might be a mite jealous about that. *Wives* can be unreasonable, *wives* can," he said, watching Semi's face.

Gayner jumped out of his chair like a jack from a box. "I guess I'll see how much snow we got last night." He grabbed his coat and was out the door before putting it on.

Semi peered through the door window before sitting down. Gayner was halfway to the barn, his coat flapping like a goose during takeoff.

Hack stood up again, walked to the gun rack, lifted down the shotgun, and returned to his chair. He bulldozed dishes away with his forearm and, making sure he had their attention, laid the gun in the cleared-off space.

"I don't like being conned," he announced. "You two haven't been straight with me."

April felt the first pang of dismay of a granddaughter about to be punished. "How do you mean, Hack?"

"You know damn well. Claiming you're man and wife."

"What makes you think we aren't?" she blustered.

But the swooping sensation in the pit of her stomach told her that the jig was up. Hack's expression was that of a prosecuting attorney with an airtight case. Semi, sitting across the table from her, raised his eyebrows and shrugged.

"I know there was never any wedding ceremony,"

Hack ranted. "I also know you've been sleeping in the same bed for two nights, so even though you weren't married before, you're sure as shootin' going to be now." He patted the gun to emphasize his choice of words.

April seized on the one part of his accusation that she could honestly deny. "We've been in the same room, but we didn't *do* anything—"

"I'm not a total fool, dammit!" Hack shut one eye and glared in a reasonable imitation of Popeye. "Now this is the plan. You, Semi Ruby, come back here next weekend with a genuine license and a genuine preacher and a genuine intention of marrying April Lynn in front of genuine witnesses—"

"Hack," April wailed, "you can't railroad him into that."

"—or you, April Lynn, can pack and move and stay off *my* property."

"Hack!"

He ignored her, squinting at Semi. "What do you say, Mr. Ruby?"

Semi leaned away and hooked an elbow on the back of his chair. He smiled at April before he smiled at her grandfather. "I've always wanted to wear a pink tuxedo."

A strange expression flitted across the old man's face—surprise tinged with dismay and, inexplicably, annoyance. Then it all smoothed into what could have passed for cordiality.

"You've just made my Christmas, son."

"Wait till I get my hands on Gayner. It has to be him. Children cannot be trusted," April grouched, striding ahead of Semi as they escaped the house for a hike in the woods.

"Whoa. You can't light into Gayner for telling your

grandfather the truth.'' He grabbed her elbow to slow her to a walk beside him.

"Oh, you're right. But now what are we going to do?'' Before Semi could answer, she stopped and grasped his jacket front to talk face-to-face. "I know what we can do. We can hire someone to play the preacher. *You* can find someone in your files.''

"No. Not on your life. We aren't going to compound our misdeeds with more underhandedness.'' She opened her mouth, and he repeated firmly, "No.''

Gently urging her forward again, Semi said, "What we're going to do is, we're going to get a genuine license and a genuine preacher and a genuine witness and be genuinely married.'' He straightened his shoulders and lifted his chin. "I'm willing to make the sacrifice.''

"No! You don't want to do that. I don't want to do that. We can't do that.''

"You sure seem positive about a lot of negative things,'' he said, putting his arm around her well-padded waist. "Think of what you'll be missing if you insist on a solitary life—no joint income tax returns, no human bed warmer on freezing nights, no two-for-the-price-of-one restaurant specials. No twenty-four-hour, full-service love.''

April laughed and shook her head, trying not to hear the truth behind his bantering.

"Hold it,'' Semi said, hauling her back and tickling her chin with a stalk of dried grass. "Don't tell me you aren't interested in having a man around to love you whenever you take the notion?''

"I've made love before,'' she admitted, knocking his hand away and dancing out of his reach. "It's overrated.''

"There's a difference between making love and

being loved," he said, suddenly serious. "Sounds like you haven't had the pleasure of the right company yet."

They walked in silence as far as the pond. Standing on the edge with her hands in her pockets, April studied the frosty scenery through the fog of her breath. Would Hack really disown her if she didn't marry? Which would be worse—life with a husband or life without her grandfather and The Shelter?

Beside her, Semi echoed her thoughts. "I guess I can understand your not wanting to marry one *particular* man. I mean, maybe I don't turn you on."

April kept her expression carefully blank, remembering that morning, when he'd very definitely turned her on.

"What I can't understand is your swearing off marriage, period. Me, I *do* want to marry. The sooner the better. Time's a-wasting." He bent to pack and hurl a therapeutic snowball at the nearest tree trunk. "And you're exactly the woman I'd hoped to find—intelligent and good-natured and great to look at—"

Disconcerted by the compliments, April swept up a double handful of loose snow and rained it at his chest.

Undistracted, Semi continued to ponder aloud. "How could I not fall for you? Love isn't something a person can control. Not even you, Ms. Independence Parish," he added, taking her arm and muscling her around the way they'd come.

The only sound for a while was their feet squeaking in the snow. April knew Semi was right about love being uncontrollable, but that was exactly why she couldn't let him—or any man—get too close. To avoid infection.

They reached the gate, and she shaded her eyes at the gray-weathered house with its sagging porch and crumbling chimneys and rusted gutters. By damn, it was worth fighting for!

She stopped Semi and grinned into his eyes. "We could get married and secretly get divorced."

"No, April," he said, like a father deeply disappointed in his child. "That would be a terrible lie. Not ivory, but ebony. I wouldn't vow wedding vows with my fingers crossed behind my back."

"People do it all the time," she protested, ashamed but too headstrong to admit it. "You're taking this too seriously."

"Maybe so, but I don't take anything for better or for worse till death do me part unless I mean it."

Linking arms with her, he started strolling toward the back porch. "Tell me one more time what you have against getting married."

April huffed an impatient sigh. "My career comes first. That wouldn't be fair to a husband or a child. I like being able to do and go and be whatever, wherever I want. Why should I give that up for the duties of a wife and mother I don't have any interest in performing?"

"There must be more to it than that."

She tried to pull away, but he tightened his elbow, snuggling her against him. Angry, she dug in her boots, making him stop and turn toward her.

"I'm afraid of making a mistake, okay? I haven't had much experience with men, what I've had wasn't all that great, and I don't want to be tricked."

"Tricked?"

"Hurt," she snapped. "I'm not talking a little heartache here, a little disappointment there. I'm talking mental and physical agony. And believe me, I'm familiar with *that*. Enough to recognize that Sherry Greene's bruises aren't from any accident."

Semi shook his head as if to clear it. "I'm sorry, I don't follow—"

"Sherry Greene looks the way my mother did half

her life till my dad walked out. Battered.'' Feeling the anger giving way to tears, April straight-armed Semi out of her way and began stamping toward the house.

She'd gone only three steps when he caught her sleeve and pulled her backward into his arms. Holding her, his exhalations warming her temple, he murmured, "I'm sorry, April. Most men aren't like that, you know."

"I know." She swallowed hard.

"I'm not like that."

She turned inside his arms and touched the tip of her cold nose to his stubbled chin. "I know." But she had to amend that. "I think." She let him see her wavering smile.

"Well?" He smiled, too. "So?"

"So check with me in a year or two when I've had analysis."

"Analysis could be good. The year or two doesn't thrill me, though."

Sighing from an abundance of regrets, April said, "It won't thrill Hack either."

SIX

Semi carried their packed suitcases downstairs and thudded them on the kitchen floor. Gayner had already deposited his duffel bag in the backseat of April's car and was now sitting beside it, obviously not interested in long farewells.

"You leaving, too?" Hack said to April as she stabbed her arms into her coat sleeves. She resented the note of hopefulness in his voice.

"There's no use my staying if I'm not willing to get married, right?"

"I'm just doing this for your own good, April Lynn." Now his voice was like a preacher's—righteous and regretful. He crossed to the hearth to poke life into the fire and eased into the rocking chair.

"I left some of my clothes upstairs because I'm not giving up, Grandfather. You and I are going to come to an agreement. I'll be back."

Truth to tell, she'd left the clothes because of a sentimental superstition that if something of hers was left in the house, she'd always return one more time. It had worked so far.

Patsy stood at the open refrigerator, apparently searching for something to torture into lunch.

"Would you like us to drop you off somewhere?" April asked her.

"Not now. I may just wait till tomorrow to leave. But that will be my—"

"Last day. I know."

"Been here ninety days," Hack declared. "And every one was her last."

Patsy leaned her pink face into the refrigerator, seemingly fascinated by the lineup of condiments.

"That's okay, Patsy," April said. "Don't ever let the old coot take you for granted. He has a tendency to do that." She glared at her grandfather before crossing the room to kiss his cool, dry temple. He smelled of fresh air and coffee. Screwing up her courage, she knelt and hugged his waist, and he patted her shoulder awkwardly.

The dining room door shivered under a knock, making everyone start.

"Come the hell in," Hack yelled, pushing April away.

Sherry Greene's pale face was first through the door, the blue-and-white bundle over her shoulder had to be Casey, and Ivan Como brought up the rear.

"Are we too early?" Sherry asked softly. "I thought maybe I could help with lunch."

Patsy, who'd been leaning on the sink watching this real, live soap opera of a crazy old man and his chip-off-the-block granddaughter, now spun around to begin peeling potatoes with a vengeance.

"Are you going somewhere?" Sherry asked, noticing the baggage Semi had just picked up. "Before Christmas dinner?"

"I'm afraid we have to get back to the city," April replied with less hauteur than she'd intended. She was suddenly picturing how lonely and cold the front rooms of the house must be to Sherry, who should be celebrating Casey's first Christmas with decorations, toys, a husband.

Semi, perhaps thinking along the same lines, set the bags down again and walked over to Sherry to peek at the baby.

"Would you like to hold him?" she offered, shyly proud.

"Sure."

His big hands shoveled the tiny body onto his own broad shoulder. April wished for her sketch pad, wanting to capture the gentle giant, his neck arched so he could gaze at the elfin face by his chin. He *ought* to be married, with children of his own, not wasting his time with a—a prospective old-maid recluse.

He swiveled his face to grin at her, and April felt a perverse pang of jealousy for the theoretical lucky woman.

"We better go," she decided. "Gayner's going to freeze, waiting for us out there."

"Yeah, right." Semi returned baby to mother with a courtly bow. "Thanks for the pleasure of his company."

Sherry giggled. She gave the baby to Ivan and slipped off her coat, preparing to help Patsy. April thought that in this case too many cooks might improve the broth.

Into the momentarily silent kitchen came the intrusive hum of a motor and the crackle of snow under tires. Shoving the baby at the closest person—April—Ivan strode across the room and made his reach-for-a-holster gesture, peering sideways out the door window in perfect imitation of a movie gangster.

Holding Casey's middle between her two hands as if she'd been given custody of a bomb, April saw a big

102 / CAROL CAIL

white car glide to a stop next to her little black one. A woman got out, bent to say something to Gayner, and opened her car's trunk to withdraw two plastic sacks overflowing with gaily wrapped parcels.

As she crossed toward the house, Ivan said, "What's your sister look like, Sherry?" and April saw the resemblance.

Sherry's face relaxed into a smile of anticipation. "An older, heavier me."

Straightening, Ivan dropped his hand.

April's arms were beginning to quiver from Casey's surprising weight. Carefully rearranging him into a sitting position, she rested him gingerly on her hip. His solemn round face tilted up to examine her, and she bit her lip in readiness for his wail. Instead, his mouth parted in a toothless grin. Delighted, April grinned back and looked around to see if Semi was witnessing her little triumph.

He gave her two thumbs-up.

This private moment went unnoticed by the others, who were watching Ivan open the door for Sherry's sister. Sherry rushed to throw her arms around the woman before she could step inside. Hugging and patting each other, they stumbled into the house, and Ivan shut the door.

"Everyone, this is my sister, Nora Shoppell," Sherry said.

Nora scarcely glanced at anyone else before swooping to take Casey from April, telling him how much he'd grown. April, mentally relieved to be physically relieved of duty, signaled Semi, *Let's go*, with her head. Turning, she intercepted a similar signal passing between Hack and Ivan.

"I'll go see what's keeping Clint," Ivan said.

"I think I'll take a walk," Hack said.

Feeling like a stranger in her own home, April announced that they were leaving and didn't wait to see if anyone noticed.

Gayner had been standing on his head in the driver's seat; when he glimpsed them coming, he fell into the back and clutched himself in an impressive show of shivering. As April put the car into reverse, Hack stepped off the porch and set out on his walk.

He had the shotgun for company.

Semi slouched sideways, his head against the passenger window, watching April drive.

He'd never be the same again. She was going to dump him at his sister's house and accelerate out of his life. He was about to experience the worst case of post-Christmas blues he'd ever had.

Mechanically sweeping the car to the left to pass a church bus, April was visualizing her beloved Shelter as a notorious refuge for outlaws, another Hole-in-the-Wall.

"Maybe my grandfather isn't just eccentric," she said out loud. "Maybe he's dangerous. Do you think he's crazy?"

When Semi didn't say yes—or anything else—she glanced sideways to see if he, like Gayner, had fallen asleep. Semi's mournful eyes glittered back at her.

"Ohmigosh," she breathed. "You do. So how am I going to protect him and the farm when he won't let me set foot on it?"

"Sorry, I was thinking about something else." Semi sat up straighter. "I don't think he's crazy," he said, reserving judgment on the old man's dangerousness.

Turning to check that Gayner was not just playing possum, he leaned closer to April to murmur, "I'm going to miss sleeping with you tonight."

"Don't distract me while I'm driving," she said.

"Why not? You distract me while I'm riding." His

hand settled lightly on her knee and, when she didn't slap it away, relaxed to stay there.

While the others sat in Hack's kitchen drinking their fourth cups of coffee, Clint was prowling the chilly front of the house, tapping the walls and scraping the toe of his shoe on warped floorboards. He didn't like being cooped up in this spooky old house in the bull's-eye of nowhere. He didn't like being without fancy food and booze and women. He especially didn't like looking over his shoulder all the time, jumping at every little noise, and not having his Smith and Wesson strapped under his arm.

Craving action and the good old days, Clint was searching for the safe he was certain Hack must have filled with . . . something. Cash would be perfect, bonds would be nice, jewels and silverware would do. A guy with a mansion this size had to have some kind of tangible assets, and Hack didn't seem the type to trust a bank.

Clint wasn't certain what he'd do if he found the goodies. Take off on his own? It would be risky, but he sure was fed up with little Ivan bossing him around. If there was *enough* in the safe, maybe he could buy himself a pardon. Yeah. He hadn't done anything too awful yet, nothing that he couldn't make up.

Hands in his pockets, Clint stopped in the doorway of the parlor and ran a practiced eye around the shabby room before going in to look behind the paintings.

With only a little help from her passengers, April found the red-porched house again. Late afternoon sun made it glow like an overheated stove.

As the car bumped over frozen ruts to the curb, Semi said, "You'll have to come in and meet my sister."

"Oh, I don't think so. Not today. Thanks anyway."

"What else have you got to do? It's Christmas Day. You don't want to be alone." His hand, which had been a warm and pleasant weight all this time, left her knee with one final squeeze.

"Okay, but just for a minute," she capitulated, shutting off the motor.

Gayner led the way to the house, showing off by carrying his and Semi's bags, which banged and staggered his legs. Semi opened the front door and they stepped into a sunny, chocolate-scented hall.

Abandoning the luggage in front of April, Gayner galloped toward the back of the house, announcing, "We're home, you guys."

Moving the bags aside, Semi touched April's elbow, indicating she should follow their herald. She was feeling something she seldom felt—shy self-consciousness. As if it mattered that these people approve of her. People she'd probably never meet again.

The door at the end of the hall led into a red-and-white kitchen alive with youngsters. Cookie-making was in progress. Every horizontal surface bore a cookie sheet or raw dough being rolled and cut. Intent faces, preoccupied by their creative tasks, scarcely glanced at April. Gayner had alrcady shed his coat to push up his sleeves and help.

"Wash up, wash up," a hearty voice reminded him. The round little woman in jeans, flannel shirt, and ruffled pinafore wiped dark hair out of her eyes with the back of a floured hand and grinned at April.

"This is my sister, Dale. Dale, April," Semi said, steering April closer.

"I won't shake hands," Dale said. "But I'm glad to meet you."

"I apologize for taking Semi away from his family at Christmas. I'm sure he'd rather have been here eating cookies."

"Don't kid yourself. He told me what a cushy job he'd got with this good-looking lady. Said it could be the start of a whole new career."

Semi, his neck rosy and getting rosier, said, "Where's Mom?"

"Watching TV. Leroy, there's plenty of room there for two of you to work. Keep your elbows to yourself."

The two biggest girls had taken an interest in April. The one with improbably electric-blue eyelashes blew a pink bubble, snapped it back into her mouth, and demanded, "You the juicy fruit who's dating Semi this week?"

"Yes, I guess I am," April admitted.

The other girl, dreamily breaking eggs into a bowl, had a softer face and an angelic smile. "Treat him sweet," she chirped. "Or your ass is grass. Doris the Enforceress has spoken."

"Right," April said. "Nice to meet you."

"Come on, we'll say hi to Mom," Semi said, increasing the pressure on her back.

"Nice to have met you," April repeated across her shoulder to Dale, who was too busy diving for an overturned flour sack to respond.

Semi took them on a circuitous path through a dining room furnished with a long table and mismatched chairs, and a living room strewn with newspapers, pillows, and an old-fashioned erector set. A plain, open staircase marched up one wall, and, under that, a gaping door emitted mournful organ music and a deep voice promising, "We will return to our story after these messages."

Semi's shoulders filled the little stairwell, leading April down. "Hey, Mom," he called ahead of them. "You decent?"

The basement had been lined with oak paneling, but otherwise it was just a basement—overhead pipes, exposed rafters, concrete floor. April found herself disappointed that none of the interior was as imaginatively decorated as the exterior of the house. Even the Christmas tree in one corner was a conventional snow-flocked artificial one, trimmed with construction-paper chains and popcorn.

An assortment of overstuffed chairs and sofas faced the television set. The only viewer was a tiny, frizzy-haired lady in a camel coat. She lounged on a brown vinyl recliner, her ankles and arms crossed. Watching their approach, she didn't smile, but she did use the remote control to soften the aspirin commercial.

"Mom, this is a very good friend of mine, April Parish. April, my mother, Wanda Ruby."

"You have such a poetic name," Mrs. Ruby said, pronouncing it slowly and with feeling. "I'm a poet, you see, so I notice things like that."

"A poet? How wonderful."

"You two have a lot in common," Semi said. "April's an artist."

Mrs. Ruby shut one eye and studied April with the other. "Yes, I can see she has a creative aura. A lovely peachy pink."

"You can see auras?" April glanced uneasily at Semi. Did he want her to encourage this eccentric notion?

"Will you sit down?" Mrs. Ruby waved at the wealth of seating available.

"No, thank you. I have to be getting on home," April said. "I just wanted to wish you a happy, happy Christmas."

"The same to you, dear. I'm sure you're good for Swinburne. He works too hard."

"Uhhh, yes," April agreed, throwing Semi a sidelong glance. "I'm sure Swinburne does."

Taking her hand to draw her away, Semi muttered under his breath, "So now you know."

The audio behind them blared and softened to a shout.

April said, " 'Swinburne' is a perfectly respectable name. After the poet, I assume?"

"Yes, and Dale is really Teasdale, after *that* poet. It could have been worse," he said, putting a foot on the first stair step. "She could have called one of us Anonymous."

Before April could laugh, Mrs. Ruby's shrill voice overrode the TV. "April! Dear! Do be careful of that enormous man with the little gun under his arm."

They looked at each other, and wordlessly retraced their path to Mrs. Ruby's chair. She beamed up at them.

"What man, Mom?" Semi asked gently. "Has there been someone here asking for April?"

"No, dear. Why would anyone do that? She's with you in Cleveland or somewhere." She waved at him impatiently to get out of her line of sight as the television heroine echoed, "Somewhere. We'll find love somewhere."

Semi disobeyed, leaning down, eye to eye, to further engage her attention. "Then how do you know about a man with a gun?"

"Mother's intuition," she said, tapping her forehead. "Now go away."

They stepped out onto the brilliant porch. From the far kitchen came Doris the Enforceress's unmistakable trill. "Cookie-baking is so hebetudinous!"

"Is your mother okay?" April asked, letting Semi help her down to the sidewalk.

"Okay?"

"I mean, she was wearing a coat, and she seemed a bit, uhhh, disoriented."

"She always wears that coat. It's her security blanket, I guess."

"Can she really see auras?"

"If there're auras to be seen, I'm sure my mom sees them."

Reaching the car, they turned to face each other.

"So how did she know about Ivan? Although she got his description wrong. 'Enormous' isn't right. How did she know about him?"

Grimacing, Semi rubbed the back of his neck with one hand. "I don't know," he admitted. "She's kind of psychic."

"Kind of— You believe that stuff?"

He shrugged, grinning. "Well, then *you* explain it."

As usual, his good humor brought out hers. Smiling, April slid into the car. Semi held the door wide while she fastened her seat belt and hunted for the key.

"Thanks for everything," she said without looking up. "You were the perfect husband."

"Hey, don't sound so final about it. Can't I see you again? How about dinner every night this week?" He rested an arm on top of the car and leaned into the door as if to keep her till she made a commitment.

"What are you, a masochist? Believe me, you don't want to be involved in the further adventures of spinster April and her weird grandsire." She prodded him out of the way and slammed the door. Through the glass she called, "I'll mail you your check tomorrow."

Semi sighed and rapped the roof with a knuckled fist before backing away so that she could leave.

" 'Bye," she shouted over the starting-up motor.

When she checked the rearview mirror, halfway down the block, he was still standing at the curb. Feeling desperately noble, she tried not to notice how bleakly the next days stretched before her.

Twenty-five minutes later, she elbowed through her own front door, a suitcase in each hand, trying to out-race a phone that had been ringing since the top ten steps to her floor.

Snatching up the receiver, she panted, "Hello?"

"Hi." Semi's warm voice tickled her ear. "God, but I've missed you."

April felt the ambiguous emotions of a Mary whose lamb wouldn't stay home.

Hack and Ivan sat at the kitchen table drinking whis-key from jelly glasses. One shot was all they were allowing themselves, Ivan for health reasons and Hack because it was his whiskey. The room was mellow with the gray light that comes just before the lamps had to be lit.

The two men carried on a desultory conversation full of thoughtful pauses. The last remark Ivan had made was that he felt sorry for Hack's granddaughter.

A full minute later, Hack gently belched and said, "She'll live. Likes to scrap and try to match wits with her old granddad. It's good for her. Gives her strength."

Ivan snickered. "I believe I heard her say those very words after a go-round with you—'Give me strength.' "

The cat under Hack's chair began to snore. The kitchen windows shivered in the wind.

"So," Ivan said, "you don't think you should just let her in on our little secret?"

Pulling at his lower lip, giving the question half a minute's consideration, Hack said, "You know as well as I do that the more people who know about us, the more dangerous it is. It's best to run her off, especially now she's got this bridegroom impersonator in tow."

The room continued to fill with shadows and silence.

"Once we get rid of Sherry," Hack speculated, "I can handle Clint by myself. You can get back to your reading. What is it now—how to write a letter bomb?"

Ivan tossed back the last of his whiskey and planted his feet to stand up. "Speaking of letters, we ought to be getting one soon. Advising on who our next victim will be."

"You have to eat supper, right?" Semi said. "I'll come get you in about an hour, and we'll go someplace quiet."

Across town, connected to him by the telephone umbilical, April shook her head wonderingly at his persistence.

Semi's voice deepened and roughened. "I'm not asking you to *marry* me tonight, just to put your lovely legs under the same table as mine. My legs, not my lovely legs. Although they aren't too bad, if I do say so myself. You still there?"

"Semi, I was looking forward to an evening to myself."

"You need to wash your hair?" he sneered.

"I need to decide what to do about Hack. My God, Ivan could be murdering him as we speak."

"Your grandfather can take care of himself, or he wouldn't have lived this long. Your worrying isn't going to help him or you. At least let me come over and help you pace the floor."

For Semi's sake, she ought to say no. For her sake, she said, "Okay, I'm hungry. Let's go someplace quiet."

When he arrived, Semi had a plastic grocery bag hanging from each hand. "I couldn't think of any place quieter than here."

She followed him into the galley kitchen to snoop

through his purchases while he washed his hands. "Where's the expensive T-bone steak? All you've got is cheap vegetables."

"Don't kid me. I've never seen you eat meat. Patsy's leather ham doesn't count."

"Where did you find a grocery open on Christmas night?"

"The Bah-Humbug on East Third. You sit over there and talk to me while I work. Feel free to parade all your fears and concerns."

Perching on the indicated stool, she folded her arms. "You said you could find out what the police have on Ivan and company."

"I've already called a reporter friend about it. He knows his way around the police department. He's going to check their names and descriptions against the arrest records and get back to me."

Semi thought it best not to mention that one of the names he'd asked to be checked was that of Hackett Jones.

April dropped her napkin on her plate and leaned back, sighing with satisfaction. "Who needs T-bone when there are omelets filled with every vegetable and cheese known to man?"

"The chef is now the busboy," Semi said, standing to gather their silverware and plates. "Everything shall be left as spotless as he found it."

"Do I detect a note of sarcasm in that remark?"

If he answered, it was lost in the clatter of the dishwasher being loaded. When the dial ratcheted and water began to gush in, Semi bustled back, a trio of videotapes in his hand. "Let me entertain you."

"What makes you think I have a VCR?"

"Everyone has a VCR." He shuffled the boxes. "Actually, I noticed it when I was here consoling you after Motormouth Meldon let you down. What's your pleasure?"

"Let me guess. You've got something steamy and sex-rated, like—*Last Tango in Paris*."

"Is that what you'd like to see?" His smile was hopeful.

"No."

He dropped one of the tapes on the table. "Okay. And behind box number two?"

"An animated movie for children—*Bambi* or *Charlotte's Web* or something. To appeal to my artistic side. And make me cry. I don't want to see that either."

He read the box in his left hand and tossed it to the table. Holding the third choice aloft, he wiggled it as if to tantalize. "Is it an exercise tape? A how-to-fix-your-car? Home movies of Gayner cleaning his room with a blow dryer?"

She laughed. "Yeah, I'd like to see that last one."

"Sorry. He did try to do that, but I don't have a camcorder." He crossed to the TV and bent to study the controls.

"It's an old movie," she guessed. *"Casablanca."*

"You're warm. You like Jimmy Stewart?"

"Yes. A Western?" she asked hopefully, moving to the sectional couch.

"A Christmas story. *It's a Wonderful Life*."

"I've heard of it."

He stabbed the movie into play and backed toward the couch himself. "It's a classic. You'll love it."

Sinking beside her with a whoosh of cushions, Semi stretched his arms either way along the backrest, one ankle on the opposite knee. He looked very natural and at ease. Very masculine. Ashamed of her weakness, April wanted, nevertheless, to lean into him and shut her eyes.

The movie score soared, and she wriggled straighter, preparing to be entertained.

Thirty minutes into the movie, April could see where it was leading. And why Semi had chosen it.

Struggling up from the couch, she raised her voice above Stewart's bewildered stammer. "I'm going to have some wine. You want any?" She paused to replace the shoes she'd slipped off.

Semi stood, too, and stopped the tape. A beer commercial leaped into the breach. Lowering the sound, he followed her into the kitchen. "So how do you like the film so far?"

Taking down two long-stemmed glasses, rearranging refrigerator contents till she found the wine bottle, she answered, "I'm not sure. It's hard to be objective about it. I keep seeing it from *your* viewpoint."

"Mine?" He took the bottle from her and squeezed the cork free. "How do you mean?"

As he reached past her to pour, the scent of his body, musky and male, filled her head.

"I mean, you expect this movie to make me see the light. Here's this fine man with his fine family, and we get to see how horrible it would have been for everyone if he'd never been born. Like, look, April, this is how sad your future is going to be if you persist in the way you're going."

"Come on, April, it's just a show—not a test." He clasped her forearms and gave her the slightest of shakes. Letting go of one side, he handed her a wineglass.

"Lots of people don't get married and still live happily ever after." Sipping, she eyed him across the rim of the glass.

"Right. Maybe there ought to be another version where Jimmy stays a bachelor and has a wonderful life as a gigolo party animal." He tasted his wine with an enthusiastic slurp and a smack of his lips.

"That's not what I want either!" Setting down the drink she didn't want after all, she walked out of his loose embrace and back to the living room.

She felt anger rising like bile, urging her to argue with him, provoke him into fighting with her. To prove she was right about lovers—would-be lovers—becoming adversaries.

Accordingly, she snarled, "I don't have to explain myself to you."

He swallowed wine and wiped his lower lip with a knuckle. "No, of course not."

" 'No, of course not,' " she mimicked. "And to yourself you're thinking what a dumb broad I am. Right? Turning down a chance to marry and be secure and adored for the rest of my life. Right? Turning down children and children's children. And joint income taxes and family insurance rates. Huh?" She kicked at the beanbag chair as she passed it, stumbled against the sofa, and sat down.

"No kidding? Insurance rates are cheaper if you've got a family?" Semi left his drink and strolled over to join her.

Standing at the end of the sectional, he folded his arms and gazed at the inaudible picture of two police-men conferring in the front seat of their cruiser. She wondered what there was about it that made him smile. Realizing he was probably amused at *her* theatrics fueled her temper.

"Go ahead, say what you're thinking," she baited him.

"I'm thinking that brand of wine is sure powerful if one sip can make you so mean drunk." He ducked reflexively. "Huh. Is that why they call them throw pillows?"

"I told you we'd fight if we were married. We fight even when we aren't married."

"You call this fighting? This isn't even an argument. It takes two to do that, and *you're* doing all the work at the moment."

"I know what you're really thinking. All you want from me is a romp in the hay."

"Hey," he warned.

"Yes. And when you get what you want, *if* you get what you want, you won't be interested in it anymore. Wham, bang, thank you, boss."

"April—"

"You and your concerned talk about marrying me. You ought to patent that particular line."

Semi's mouth opened and snapped shut before the reprisal could escape. His eyes glittering, he took a giant step closer.

Staring up at him, at his looming torso, the muscles that flexed in his jaw, and his fisted hands, April held her breath, bracing herself—waiting for him to lash out at her and prove her right.

SEVEN

He didn't hit her. What he did was reach out a careful hand to cradle her chin as his smoke-soft voice told her, "You can't drive me away with your ivory anger."

Something heavy inside April's chest began to melt and dissolve in the heat of his regard. Ignoring the sensation of buoyancy—of freedom from past misconceptions—she made herself say, "If you value your life, Semi, leave now and don't come back."

His eyes stared into hers as if he could read her mind through them. Sinking to sit beside her, still touching her face, he enunciated each word with care. "I think I love you, April. I want you to marry me."

However her father had proposed to her mother, April was sure he would never have expressed anything but positive, unequivocal, undying love. Her mouth twisted with wry amusement. "You *think* you love me?"

The serious Semi smiled and became his easygoing self. "I was never in love to know what it feels like. Unless it was with Mindy Celeste Gandyshire in the fourth grade." He eased his arms around her as if afraid of spooking her and, cheek against her temple, whispered, "You want to watch the rest of the movie?"

She gave a mirthless laugh. "I'm not sure what the hell I want."

Semi's palm stroked up her shoulder blade and massaged the base of her neck. Gradually she relaxed against him, feeling safe. Cherished. It was an unfamiliar, wonderful feeling.

They held one another, their eyes shut. The television muttered and a jet plane rumbled overhead. While Semi's breathing stirred her hair, April rested her face against his throat and sighed with contentment.

Then she laughed.

"What's so funny?"

"Poor Semi. Falsely accused by my grandfather of fooling around with me. And on top of that, you haven't been paid the wages you've earned."

"Money isn't everything is what I hear," he said, slowly reclining their combined weight against the sofa back.

"*Nothing* is *everything*."

"Hmm. No, I'd argue that love is everything. There's nothing that can't be put right—or at least improved—by honest love." He slid his fingers into her hair, cupping the back of her head. "For instance, I've been thinking about what you said about analysis. You were probably kidding, but—"

April's contentment drained away. She stiffened, and Semi's arms corralled her in an unbreakable embrace.

"Shh, no, listen," he reassured her. "I want to be your therapist."

"I think my hang-ups are too ingrained for a career counselor to—"

"No, not the professional me, the personal me," he said, not letting her struggle free. "The me that cares for you. I want to kiss your hurts and make them better.''

"Sure,'' she joked to hide how this touched her. "Everybody wants to be a sex therapist.''

He sighed the exaggerated sigh of a misunderstood man.

Impulsively, April stretched to kiss the corner of his turned-down mouth. His face twisted to welcome her, and his wine-scented breath was warm on her lips. Then he was kissing her, mouth open and demanding, making her stomach somersault with desire.

Even with her eyes shut, April sensed the room whirling around her, and every sound was magnified— her heartbeat, Semi's palms kneading her shoulders, their labored breathing. The tide of sexuality swept her out of herself, and she clung to Semi as if he were a lifeline.

He broke off the kiss, rustled away from her, helped her sit straighter. She waited for him to take off his shirt. Or her shirt. Wanted him to.

Instead, he showed her a wobbly smile and got to his feet. "Sorry. I better go while the going's not only good but still possible.''

She meant to feel relieved. She ought to be grateful that he had enough willpower to put the brakes on their runaway desire.

What she did feel was unadulterated disappointment.

Standing, she tipped back her head and ran both hands through her hair, wishing that the gesture was too provocative for Semi to resist touching her again.

He turned away, wondering out loud where he'd put his jacket.

"Semi, wait,'' she blurted before she could think better of it. "What you said about helping me work through my fear of marriage—what did you have in mind?''

Startled, he swung around and saw that she was serious. "I just think . . . if you and I proceed as if we're really going to be married next weekend, maybe you'll find out you *want* to. After you get to know me better."

April smiled ruefully. "Yeah, and maybe after you get to know *me*, you'll find out you *don't* want to." She stepped forward impulsively and gave him a quick, hard hug, her nose buried in the hollow of his neck.

He kept her there, his arms a warm vise. "I already know all I need to know about you."

She leaned back to eye him skeptically. "All?"

"Enough."

"How can I love a guy who would fall in love with a woman the likes of me?" she mock-scolded.

He touched his forehead to hers in brief affirmation. "So you want to get a wedding license tomorrow? Just in case?"

Feeling the way a novice parachutist must when stepping into the sky, she whispered, "What time?"

At two-thirty the next day, April sat in a plush purple chair, watching Semi being fitted for a wedding suit.

"Just in case," he said, winking at her in the multiview mirror.

She nodded, bemused by the sight of the saleswoman—a brisk but attractive redhead—embracing his middle with a tape measure.

Lunch had been sub sandwiches at a no-frills coffee shop—peanut butter wasn't a choice on the menu. Next they'd taken April's car to the courthouse and picked up the marriage license—no waiting period required in Montgomery County. And now they were in this quiet nook of a men's shop off Third Street, listening to a symphonic version of "Only the Good Die Young," choosing Semi a suitable suit.

"Is gray okay?" he asked as he slipped into the

jacket Red was holding out and shrugged to settle it on his wide shoulders.

"You'd better buy whatever color you'll wear for occasions other than weddings," April cautioned.

He stretched his arms, checking the length of the sleeves. "Look at this," he said proudly, jacket open, hands on hips, back straight as the Jolly Gray Giant.

April looked, not sure what he wanted her to admire, but finding her own particular favorites among the sites offered.

"A whole waist size smaller," he elaborated. "I can write a how-to-reduce book now. Eat light, exercise, and chase women who don't want to be married." He held his breath and patted his stomach.

"Semi, I don't know why you're so worried about your weight. You're a great-looking guy."

"Yeah?" He leaned forward to take another look in the mirror, his face a pleased pink. "Well, so gray would go with anything, right? What color wedding dress would you be wearing?"

"I would probably not be wearing any."

"My favorite color." He showed her his shy smirk.

The saleslady gave each of them a quick, interested glance before she knelt to measure Semi's inseam.

Watching, April felt an irrational urge to slap the woman's hand away.

Within the hour, their roles reversed, Semi sat in the silver brocade chair of a perfumed and hushed women's shop, admiring four Aprils as she inspected her reflection. She'd tried on six dresses, and he'd liked them all. She'd been more critical. The one she was considering now was a splashy pink, green, and beige floral. The short puffed sleeves, dropped waist, and full skirt would have made most women look like fruit baskets. On April's tall, slender body, it was perfect.

"Perfect," Semi said.

"Think so?" She smoothed a palm down her stomach, sighting over one shoulder at the fit.

"It's very becoming," the white-haired saleswoman said. "Is it for a special occasion?"

"No," April said, giving Semi a severe look.

Ralph Greene had followed Sherry's sister, Nora, to The Shelter and seen her leave again late Christmas Day. Alone.

Since then, he'd camped in the blind he'd made of evergreen boughs in the woods across the road. Stiff from the cold and the inactivity, he waited for a glimpse of his wife. Living on candy bars and pop, he waited for proof that she was in the run-down mansion. As his misery increased, his certainty grew. Sherry was over there, enjoying heat and gourmet food and a feather bed.

He wasn't going to be patient much longer.

Semi arrived to take April to dinner that night in, appropriately, a pickup truck. She expressed doubt about his story that "the Porsche is in the garage." They went to a new seafood place that was slow on service but worth the delay.

As they feasted on buttery lobster and crisp slaw, April asked, "Have you heard from your friend who's looking up the police information for us?"

"Not yet. I'll call you as soon as he calls me."

"I phoned The Shelter this afternoon. Patsy answered, but I didn't ask if it was her last day. Hack was as sociable as a terrorist with a plane to catch. In other words, everything seemed normal."

Semi reached across the table to gently swipe the corner of her mouth with his thumb. "Melted butter. What else did you do after you took me back to work?"

"Began some sketches *Tiny People* magazine commissioned. They aren't due for a couple of months, but this gives me a head start."

"Umm-hmm." He chewed, swallowed, and pointed at her bare left hand, cupped around her iced tea glass. "You know, something else we should do is buy a wedding ring."

"I have one, remember?"

"But I don't."

"Oh, yeah. How late do the discount marts stay open?"

Semi could tell she was growing more comfortable with him every day, and she probably thought she knew him well by now. It was time to unsettle her complacency.

He knew how to do it, too. He just didn't *want* to do it. What she needed was some time alone to think about and miss him. Accordingly, when they left the restaurant at nearly ten, he took her straight home, walked her as far as the front porch, and told her goodnight.

"You aren't going to beg and grovel to come up?" she said.

She *did* know him well, he thought ruefully. "Not this time, sorry," he said with an air of injured dignity. "I will take a farewell kiss, if you'd be so kind."

Stepping into his arms, she tilted her face to meet his, her lips warm and garlicky, her smoky-lidded eyes shut as if to savor him. He ached to change his mind, march in lockstep upstairs with her, reprise last night, and this time stay to the logical conclusion.

But "beg" and "grovel" stung his pride, and he let her go.

She rested her hand on his cheek before turning away and disappearing inside.

Climbing the stairs to her apartment, April was thinking back to their dinner and the drive home, wondering what she'd done or said to make him rush away like this. Not that she wasn't relieved. Of course she was.

She stabbed key into lock, snapped on the living room light, and slumped onto the couch, trying to remember if she'd used deodorant after her shower.

Semi, singing along with a golden oldie on his truck radio, would have been pleased to see his plan working.

April was annoyed the next morning to find herself waiting for Semi to phone her. Setting up her easel and examining yesterday's preliminary sketch, she realized she'd given Digby Pig Semi's smirky grin.

What was she going to do about Semi? Should she stick to her plan of being single, or should she race him to the altar and hope for the best?

There must be dozens of eligible women he could choose from, women who'd marry him in a minute and never give him reason to regret it.

But he said he wanted her. In spite of her independent nature. Or maybe because of it? Did he want her because she was so hard to get? Would he lose interest if she allowed him to catch her?

Throwing up her hands in helpless disgust, April flounced to turn the radio on full blast and drown out her worries with infectious rock and roll.

When the phone did ring, she switched off the music and answered mechanically, narrowing appraising eyes at the nearly finished picture.

"I'm not begging or groveling, just asking. You want to have dinner with me?"

"Hi, Semi." She tucked the phone into her shoulder to scrub at her hands with a dry rag. "Come over. I'll order a pizza."

"What kind of movie should I bring?"

"No movie. I'll provide the entertainment," she said, grinning.

After a moment of interested silence, he ventured, "You will?"

"I've got a deck of cards around here somewhere," she said with wicked brusqueness. "See you."

Later, while the hot shower spray kneaded her back, she made up her mind. One thing she could say with absolute certainty—she wanted to make love to Semi. Tonight she would put all her worries on hold and enjoy his company—to the *hilt*, if he'd let her! Laughing at the image she'd conjured, she toweled her skin till it glowed.

Ralph Greene had intended to cross the road and lay siege to The Shelter today, but instead he'd huddled in the down sleeping bag, alternating between chills and fever, too weak to think, let alone act. His dreams were full of red-and-green totems that loomed over him chanting, "Flu, flu."

When he woke to a ghostly quarter moon, he told it, "That's right. She flew."

The virus was twenty-four-hour. Sherry's escape might be forever.

Gritting his teeth, Ralph pawed through the debris around him till he found the binoculars and, ignoring his headache, began to watch again.

"Did your reporter friend call you today?" April licked tomato sauce from her thumb and reached for another slice of pizza.

Semi shook his head, chewed, and swallowed. "If he doesn't phone me in the morning, I'll call him and ask for some action."

"I do hate sitting here wondering what's happening at the farm. How long do you suppose Hack's been renting rooms to the likes of Ivan Como?'' It was a rhetorical question, and she didn't wait for a theoretical response. ''I'm to blame. I shouldn't have stayed away so much.''

''Hack's his own boss. He'd have done whatever he wanted, whether you were there or not.''

They sat cross-legged on opposite sides of the coffee table, the pizza rapidly disappearing between them. MTV flickered at their shoulders, the volume turned low. In clean jeans and a black turtleneck sweater, underarms daubed more than once with roll-on deodorant, April tingled with suppressed excitement.

Semi's hand, reaching for his can of beer, detoured to pat the wrist she had rested on the table. ''Don't blame yourself.''

She frowned, trying to recall the topic of conversation. Hack.

''And I'm not too sure he'd be any happier seeing you married, either,'' Semi continued. ''He's probably happiest when he's verbally sparring with you. If you kowtowed to everything he demanded, he wouldn't be so fond of you.''

''You think he's fond of me?'' she asked wistfully. ''He's sure never said so.''

''He's not a demonstrative man. I bet he didn't tell his wife he loved her very often.''

April slumped, momentarily struck with pity for the grandmother she hadn't known. ''I'm afraid you're right.''

''I, on the other hand,'' Semi said, ''would make a daily point of showing my mate in many little ways how much I loved her.''

Eyes glinting with mischievous daring, April said, ''Many little ways, huh? No big, big ways?''

Ignoring the possibly double entendre, Semi popped

a last bite into his mouth and crumpled up his napkin. "Bring on the cards."

"I forgot to hunt them up." She hauled herself upright and collected their trash. "You want to help me look?"

"Where should I start?" he asked the back of her head as she started toward the kitchen with her hands full. His eyes slid down to appreciate the tight grip her jeans had on her bottom.

"Try the bedroom," was her airy answer.

"Uhh, I better not," he said. "You might have left some embarrassing, lacy black nothing draped over the lampshade."

Surprised—and a little hurt—that he didn't jump at the opportunity she'd offered him, April snapped the tabs off two beers and brought them back with her. Handing Semi one, she slid down to sit behind him, leaning back-to-back.

After several minutes of companionable silence, Semi twisted around, one arm lifted, to haul her to his chest. Tilting her face to his kiss, April sighed and relaxed. As before when he embraced her, Semi's arms felt both strong and gentle. Then stronger and less gentle, as he gathered her closer and fastened his mouth demandingly on hers.

Excitement spreading through her blood, she moaned against his lips and found one of his hands to drag to her breast. His touch, even through her clothing, made her vibrate with pleasure. She fumbled with the waistband of her sweater, making an entrance for him.

"No," he breathed against her mouth. "You don't want—"

"I *do* want. Come on, Semi. Let's just let go and do what"—she nibble-kissed him—"ever . . ." Trailing kisses down his throat, she finished, ". . . comes naturally."

"Oh, God, April. Don't tease me."

"I've never been more serious." Twisting the top buttons of his shirt out of their buttonholes, she pressed her hot cheek into the wiry nest below his collarbone. Patting down his front to the buckle of his belt, she began to work it free.

"April!" He leaned away and gripped both of her wrists. "Do you know what you're doing? You're driving me crazy."

"Good." She smiled into his eyes.

"No. Not good," he said sternly.

His expression was so forbidding, her euphoria slipped away like quicksilver. "I'm sorry," she said in a small, contrite voice. "Am I being too aggressive?"

"I love it. As you can see." He nodded at himself. "If you don't stop, I won't be able to."

In answer, she shook her wrists out of his grip and, sitting on her heels, drew the sweater over her head. When her face was free of the bulky wool, she bent forward to drop butterfly kisses on his chest. His hands began to stroke her bare back.

"April, do you trust me not to hurt you?"

She let him see her smile. "I trust you to make me feel grrreat."

And he did. There on the living room rug, Semi was as slow and careful about his lovemaking as April had imagined he would be. Because he was afraid of losing control too soon, he waited till she was literally shuddering with impatience before he lifted her on top of him and let her journey past the point of no return.

When he, too, collapsed, sated and panting, she hugged him to her, thinking that he could never hurt her more than if he were to walk out of her life.

He carried her into the bedroom and they made love again to the murmuring of distant traffic.

Much, much later Semi said, "Ahhh, April, you

can't imagine how I've ached to lie with you like this. With nothing between us. No covers, no pajamas, no curtain rod.''

Snickering, she stroked his leg with hers. "Ahhh, Semi. Did I really once say that lovemaking is overrated?''

She woke when Semi twisted from under her, jarring the bed.

"What time is it?" he mumbled. "One-thirty. Drat.''

"What's the matter?" Her mouth felt full of corduroy. "You missing David Letterman?''

"I gotta go to work tomorrow.'' He swung his legs over the side of the mattress and sat up.

She stopped him, throwing both arms around his middle. "Stay with me tonight.''

He reached back to gently scrub her cool flank. "I can't do that.''

Struggling up, she stretched to nip his ear before murmuring into it, "This bed will never be the same again without you in it. To say nothing of my living room floor! Move in with me. Come live with me and be my love.''

His arms encircled and drew her forward into his chest. "Are you asking me to marry you?''

"I didn't say that.'' Even now she found herself drawing back from that final commitment.

"Live with you but don't marry you?''

"Right,'' she said brightly. "Is that a terrific offer or what?''

"It's what.''

"What?'' She giggled nervously, feeling his body tense to pull away.

"No,'' he said, and repeated it more resolutely. "No. Thanks, but no, thanks.''

The laughter gurgled dry in her throat. "You don't want to sleep with me every night?''

"God, yes, I want to sleep with you every night!" He thrust her away from him and stood up.

"Well, then, what's the problem?" she demanded, hugging the quilt to her breasts in poor substitution for his embrace.

"No problem, just a difference in outlook." His voice was muffled by the T-shirt he was dragging over his head. Pulling it down past his ribs, he said, loud and clear, "You're opposed to marrying me and I'm opposed to shacking up with you."

April sucked in a startled breath. "Did you say shacking up? Shacking up! I'm not some bimbo you met in a bar. It isn't just sexual titillation here. I care for you."

His quiet answer floated across the space between them. "And I love you."

His expression and the words sent her stomach into a slow, joyous roll. Excited, she hitched herself up onto her knees.

"Semi, that's it! The perfect solution to my phobia about marriage. Lots of people live together instead of getting married."

"It may be *your* perfect solution. Please don't lump me with 'lots of people.' " He was buttoned and zipped now, and he sat down on the edge of the bed to put on his socks and shoes. "You didn't really expect me to be thrilled and honored by your invitation, did you? I have to set a good example for the kids, after all."

"I'm not asking you to commit murder or rob a bank!" She ran a frustrated hand through her hair and left it clutching the top of her head. "Living together is no big deal."

"It is to me. And don't disparage my belief that a couple should be married before they move in together. I don't disparage your fear of matrimony."

"You sure know how to make me sound like a

bitch,'' she cried, falling onto her back and yanking the quilt up to her chin.

He stared down at her, his mouth quirked in sad amusement. ''This still isn't fighting, April Lynn.'' Patting the quilt in the vicinity of her knee, he whispered ''Good night,'' stood up, and left her.

Even after the distant snap of the front door told her the coast was clear, she was too stubborn to cry.

Clint let himself through the dining room door, walking softly in his socks, carrying a penlight that needed new batteries. He'd listened to the snoring through Ivan's closed bedroom door before slipping away in the darkness. Everyone else would be snoring, too, at two o'clock in the morning.

Gliding into the kitchen, he swept the light across the floor, reconnoitering for cats. He reached the counter where the old-fashioned black phone sat, shut off the light, and dialed from memory.

After seven rings, a bass voice full of sleep and irritation grunted, '' 'Lo.''

''It's me, Clint,'' he whispered close to the mouthpiece. ''I want to cut a deal.''

The voice was suddenly alert and all business. ''You are dead. Dead, my friend.''

''No, no. Just listen, will you? I want to make it all up.''

''Where are you?''

''In a minute. First, you got to hear my plan.''

''I don't have to hear nothing from you.''

''Just listen, will you, Dusty? They grabbed me and been holding me against my will here. Putting out all kinds of lies. You got to come get me out.''

Clint wished he'd found a safe full of valuables to shore up his position. Still, he thought the kidnapping story sounded good. When Dusty asked again, "Where are you?" Clint began to give directions.

The second *Tiny People* sketch was going badly.

April had been up since six that morning working on it, and now, at noon, she crumpled the latest version to join a wastebasket full of other failures. Too keyed up to want lunch, she smoothed paper on the drawing board for a new attack.

How could she work when all she could think about was Semi? She'd never expected to let any man get close enough to seriously affect her life. How had this one, at first appearance so ordinary and unromantic, captured her in his orbit like a sun attracting a planet?

One moment she was determined never to talk to him again, and the next moment she was ready to jettison all her life's goals if only she could be his woman forever.

April rubbed her eyes and began to draw again, but her pencil's stroke went awry as the telephone rang. For the umpteenth time, she wished she had the spare money for an answering machine.

"Hello," she said, prepared to give some salesperson short shrift.

"April, it's me."

Semi's low voice made her eyes close with longing, but her response was briskly impersonal. "Hi. What's on your mind?"

"My reporter buddy called."

Interest warmed her voice. "Great. What did he find out?"

"Nothing on Sherry or Ivan. Wait a second."

She listened impatiently to him telling a co-worker, presumably, that "it" was "in the top drawer." Then his voice was loud in her ear. "Clint Ajax has a long record, been in prison a couple of times. The rumor is he's affiliated with organized crime.''

''I knew it!'' she berated herself inaccurately. It had been Ivan she'd suspected, but with Clint for a friend, he must be guilty of something. ''Hang up. I'm calling the police.''

''On what grounds? Clint isn't doing anything illegal that you know of. There's no warrant out on him currently.''

She hesitated in her search for the phone book. ''You know that for a fact?'

''My friend asked. And anyway, you don't want to incur the wrath of your grandfather.''

At his end of the conversation, Semi was thinking that he still didn't trust Hack not to be involved in his renters' shady activities, though the old man wasn't in the police computer.

''I'm going back to the farm,'' April decided, already shaking her hair free of the red bandanna that was part of her working costume.

''You mean right away? No, listen, don't do that. Wait till this evening and I'll drive up there with you.''

''No need. Thanks all the same.'' She hunched over the phone cradle, ready to disconnect.

''April! If these guys are up to something, you could be in real danger. You need me to—''

''I'll be fine. I'll call you in a few days. To let you know I'm okay.'' She hung up and, thoughtful, left her hand on the receiver.

It would be easy to give in to weakness, to call Semi back and say, ''I need you.'' Which was exactly why she wouldn't do it.

She began unbuttoning her shirt with one hand and untying a sneaker with the other, feeling like her old, capable self.

*   *   *

As soon as Semi turned into April's street, he knew she was gone. The little black Honda was nowhere in evidence.

Nevertheless, he had to run upstairs and knock, to be doubly sure. Taking the risers two at a time, he leaned on her door and pounded with his fist. When he stopped to listen, the only sound was his own breathing.

He pounded again, listened again, and then hurtled down the steps and out to his badly parked pickup. He'd go home and pack a bag and follow her north. His employer wasn't going to like or understand it. But Semi had never been irresponsible before; he thought he was entitled to be now.

His biggest worry at the moment was whether he could retrace the right back roads to find The Shelter.

EIGHT

Driving alone through the rolling Ohio countryside, in good weather on a dual highway, April was having plenty of time to think.

First she planned what she'd say to Hack about Clint. Maybe her grandfather didn't know about the prison record, but she bet he did. She could just hear Hack scoffing that he could take care of himself and the homeplace, that Clint might have been in trouble in the past, but now he was trying to straighten out his life and needed a place to live as much as anyone else.

Then she pictured the scene when Hack found out that she and Semi still hadn't agreed to marry. There'd be snide remarks on Hack's part, some whining on hers, and either he'd throw her out again or she'd talk him into a resentful truce. Boy, did she dread it.

How was she going to protect her crusty old grandsire and her own interests in the farm? Maybe she could become one of his renters, too. She could certainly sketch and paint at The Shelter as readily as she could in the Dayton apartment. After all, that was where she meant to be eventually, in the far distant future.

This germ of an idea took root and flourished for the next many miles, so that by the time she was jouncing over secondary roads, she was deciding how soon to begin packing and which rooms in the mansion she'd want.

Having mentally settled all the little details of relocation—ignoring the big detail of whether Hack would let her—she traveled the last ten miles in sad contemplation of Semi. If she lived this far away from him, maybe they'd both decide that they should go their separate ways, that what they'd shared was only an infatuation.

Did infatuation leave such a dull ache in one's core? Ironic, how she hadn't wanted him at first, for fear he'd hurt her, and now, when it seemed she'd "won," her pain was as chronic as a disease.

Patsy was in the kitchen filling a scrub bucket at the sink. She welcomed April with "You aren't supposed to be here yet."

Dropping her one suitcase by the stair door and balancing her shoulder bag on top of it, April said, "Where's Hack?"

"Out. In the woods, I think, getting kindling. I haven't got your room ready. You weren't supposed to be back yet."

"So you said. What's wrong with the room? It was fine the way we left it." She lifted the porcelain coffeepot and found it empty.

"Hack said I should sweep out the blue room in case we needed a honeymoon suite."

April's stomach tickled with happy surprise. For a few seconds, she indulged in a daydream of spending nights in the blue room with Semi. In the front wing, it was the largest bed-sitting room and adjoining bath in the house, the master's bedroom when the house had been new. Many a day she'd spent reading there, lying on the carved oak bed or on the odd, half-backed "fainting couch," pretending to be a fine Victorian lady.

"I was just about to start cleaning it today," Patsy continued to grumble. "Had to change my plans about leaving, because it'd take at least two days to do it right."

"Don't bother," April said stiffly. "My grandfather was pulling your leg. He didn't even know for sure we'd be back."

Patsy shifted from foot to foot, frowning at this revelation. "Well, what did he want to cause me extra work for?"

"Maybe to give you a reason to stay another day," April said, slipping out of her coat.

Muscling the scrub bucket out of the sink, Patsy began to stagger across the kitchen. "If the old man wants me to do busywork, I'll do busywork. It's his dollar." She chuckled without smiling. "And I do mean dollar."

"You could at least fetch the water from the other kitchen. It's closer." April opened the stair door for Patsy. "Or are those people still using it, Ivan and Clint and What's-her-name?" she asked with offhand casualness.

Patsy grunted, hauling her burden two-handed and sideways up the steps. "I don't keep track of other people's business," she shouted down, and then contradicted herself by saying, "I think the men went somewhere today."

Sighing her displeasure that the problem of the renters had not conveniently disappeared, April picked up the coffee canister and pried off the lid.

From the top of the stairs came a yelp and the smack of water on the floor.

"There's a faucet in the blue room bathtub you can use, for gosh sake," April yelled into the stairwell.

The sound of Patsy's slow shuffle died away, and April, having finished measuring coffee and drawing water, turned to look around the kitchen. Two cats dozed in a sunlight stripe on the warped floor. The dish drainer held two cups, two saucers, two spoons, two knives, and one rusty cast-iron skillet. Beside the cold fireplace, the Christmas tree drooped, like a tired old lady in tawdry finery, all dressed up with no place to go.

It had all looked so much better when Semi was here with her.

April pulled out a dusty kitchen chair, sank into it, and put her face in her hands, preparing to let depression have its way with her.

If the men are gone, now would be the perfect time to snoop around their rooms.

Jumping up, she went to see.

Since nothing looked familiar now that he had left the interstate, Semi pulled into a gas station on a country crossroads to ask directions. The proprietor had a butch haircut, oil-stained overalls, and a cigarette cough, so Semi was startled when the customer just ahead of him left with a shout of "Take it easy, Mary."

Hating to ask advice without buying something, Semi picked up a pack of gum. "Do you know a farm around here called The Shelter?"

Mary's voice matched the cough, deep and raw. "Sure. The Jones place."

"How do I get there?"

"You know where Miller Road is? The gravel pit? The old stone church?" As he kept shaking his head, she ripped a paper towel off the nearby rack and dug a ballpoint pen out of her bib pocket.

After she'd gouged a map into the toweling for him, he was happy to learn he was only about five miles from his destination. "Do you happen to know Hack Jones?" he asked, folding one stick of spearmint into his mouth.

"I know *of* him." She crossed her arms and leaned back on her heels, eyeing Semi with suspicion.

"See, I'm an accountant," Semi invented. "He's asked me to do some work for him, and I just wondered how he'd be to work for. What kind of reputation does he have for, umm, being fair and, umm, square?"

She mulled it over. "You know the kind of person who worries about other people's problems and wants to cure the world's ills?"

Semi nodded, beginning to be relieved that his impression of the old man was wrong.

"Well, Hack's just the opposite."

Wishing she hadn't taken off her coat, April tiptoed along the threadbare hall. At least this way she could blame the shivering on being cold, instead of on her being a cowardly Nancy Drew.

Realizing that the quiet approach was wrong if she wanted to avoid surprising or being surprised, she squared her shoulders and marched to the first door. Rapping on it smartly, she called, "Ivan?"

There was nothing but creaking silence.

Moving on to check the two other doors, also closed, she shouted again, "Anybody in there?"

Apparently not. After a decent two seconds, April tried Sherry's door. It was locked.

Maybe she *was* in there.

Then why wasn't she answering?

After wasting several seconds contemplating the unhelpful knob, April rushed back to try Ivan's door. It swung open promptly, spilling her into the dim room.

Bracing herself against the wall, she felt for the light switch.

The bed, neatly made, was covered with sheets of play money, black-and-white bills, several to a page. Bending over to study the array, she decided it was all twenty-dollar bills, all bearing the same serial number, and not play money but unfinished counterfeit.

Her mouth pinched with disapproval, she considered what to do. Telephone the police to come see this blatant evidence of Ivan's criminality? Would they get here in time—before Ivan came home to cover his tracks? Would she get her grandfather in trouble by snitching? If Clint had mob connections, maybe she'd be exposing herself and Hack to reprisals.

Putting off a decision, she retreated into the hall and twisted the doorknob to Clint's room. It, too, was unlocked. Before going in, she stomped to the foot of the front stairs to shout "Sherry? Hack? Anyone?" Encountering only the mausoleum hush of a big, empty house, she returned the way she'd come and let herself into Clint's quarters.

The room looked and smelled the same as last time. Like a minor explosion in an underwear-and-tobacco warehouse. The bed was neatly made, with a crazy quilt instead of money for the top layer. Crossing to the open walk-in closet, April wrinkled her nose at the contents—one shiny black jacket and pair of pants, one shirt with a whisker-abraded collar.

Taking a step back to peer up at the shelf, she froze, wondering if she'd heard a voice. Slipping to the outer door and into the hall, she listened. "Hello? Sherry?"

No answer.

She went back to her search, not certain of what she hoped to find. There was nothing else in the closet. Nothing in the bureau drawers except more underwear. She had just lifted the bed pillows and found nothing under them when the hall door whispered wider and a floorboard squealed.

Swallowing hard, clutching one fat pillow to her chest, she choked out, "Clint?"

The man who bent from the waist to peek around the door and into the room was no one April had ever seen before.

In spite of Mary's map, Semi had made a wrong turn somewhere. Disgusted to be so disoriented, he nosed the pickup onto the shoulder of a hilltop and squinted in all directions. Several miles away on his right was a woods near a big expanse of roof. He put the truck in gear and drove right at the first crossroads for a closer look.

"Who are you?" April demanded, throwing down the pillow and folding her arms militantly.

"Ralph. Who are you?" he said, just as militantly. He had the advantage of a stereotypical sergeant's physique—muscular and squat. Or maybe it was the camouflage coveralls and the aviator cap jammed down over his ears that evoked thoughts of armed conflict.

Straightening to her full seventy-two inches, April felt like a lion about to defend territory.

"This is my house," she said, haughtiness taking up the slack in truth. "What can I do for you?"

He took off his ski gloves and blew into his hands. "*Your* house, huh? So you know what-all goes on here, right?" He ripped off the cap and threw it at the bed. His frizzy red hair sprang free, making him two inches taller. He still had to look up at April. "So where's my wife?"

Sherry's husband! This man was the abusive "accident" that Sherry was recovering from. April was sure of it.

So now what should she do? Stalling, she echoed, "Wife?"

"Sherry," he answered, impatience whining in his voice.

"There's no Sherry here, and if you don't leave the house at once, I'll have to phone the police," April said, walking briskly toward him as if expecting him to let her out of the room.

Instead, he fastened a cold, callused hand on her wrist and breathed bad air into her face. "If there's no Sherry here, then how come I found my way to this room by following your caterwauling for Sherry?"

"Well, because," April floundered, wanting to hold her nose. Ralph's aroma was more complex than a simple failure to brush his teeth. "That's the point. She isn't here. She didn't answer. She's left for good. Never coming back. I just wanted to be sure."

Dismissing this with a pithy obscenity, Ralph said, "You're as big a liar as she is. I been across the road for three, four days. If she'd left, I'd of seen. 'Less—" His expression slipped into uncertainty for all of two seconds. "Naw, I wasn't sick that long. She's got to be here."

He'd been camping across the road for half a week? No wonder the man smelled like a sewer. As he continued to drone on about Sherry, April, and faithless females in general, April twisted her arm ineffectually.

She was beginning to regret her willfulness in not waiting for Semi to come to the farm with her. He'd be at his office right now, doing busywork for complete strangers, when April could certainly put his time to better use here.

Ralph's voice stopped on an interrogative upswing, and she had no idea what he'd just asked.

While she tried to think of a noncommittal, noninflammatory response, he gave her wrist a shake and repeated, presumably, "Which room is hers?"

"Upstairs," she answered without hesitation. "Let go and I'll show you." Sherry might be a gun moll, but April wasn't going to betray her to this Neanderthal jerk.

To April's surprise, Ralph did let go, and moved aside for her to lead the way. As every step took them farther from Sherry's room and the second kitchen, the most likely places for her to be hiding if she'd heard Ralph, April said as loudly as she dared, "So, Ralph, how did you find out she was living here?"

"Easy. Followed her sister out on Christmas."

"Is that right, Ralph?" She walked fast as an excuse to be yelling over her shoulder.

Although she hadn't listened to his every word, she was certain he hadn't once asked about his baby son. Ralph was collecting black marks in her book, right and left.

She was flying up the stairs so fast, she hit the wall at the top before staggering off toward the back hall. Trying not to contemplate what he'd say or do when Sherry wasn't up here, either, she shouted, "Then how did you get in the house without someone seeing you, Ralph?"

"I just walked up the lane and in the back door. No problemento."

She skidded to a stop by the door to the bedroom she and Semi had shared. "This is it. But she's not here. She's gone and she's not coming—"

"I know, I know," he said and reached to unlatch the door and push her in ahead of him.

The room was, indeed, deserted. Even the mattress had been stripped down to its blue-and-white ticking underwear.

Flapping her arms, April said, "See?"

He prowled the room, opening the closet door, sticking his head into the bathroom. When he was that far away from her, April scuttled toward the outer door.

"Hold it!" he barked, pointing at her. It was only a finger, but it looked lethal.

She folded her arms and glared at him. "You aren't satisfied? Sherry is not—*not*—here."

He sidestepped to hold aside the window curtain and peek out.

Boy, could I use a good guidance counselor, April thought. *Someone who'd know what to say to this, this persona non grata to make him leave.*

Well, Semi isn't here, she scolded herself. *Are you a woman or a mouse?*

"Okay, buster, out," she ordered. "Now. Or I'm calling the sheriff."

"You can't. I cut the telephone line." Fishing in his coverall pocket, he produced a pocket knife and twiddled it at her.

For one quick intake of breath, she was afraid. Then she felt anger rising like sap in a tree. "That's it, then. You better get out fast, before I find my grandfather and his shotgun."

"Oooh, you're scaring me. I've seen that old man. He's big and ugly. And real, real old." Underlining his meaning with a nasty smile, he sat on the bed and began to clean his nails with the knife.

She whirled toward the hall door, ready to stomp out and slam it in his face.

"Ah-ah-ah," he said, this time pointing the knife. "You stay right here. You're stuck with me till Sherry comes back or you tell me where she's gone."

Flouncing across the room in the opposite direction, April admonished herself to think. What would Semi— or any man—do? She could do it, whatever it was. She didn't need Semi or Hack or Ivan with his shoulder holster.

That thought dislodged another one, a memory of Semi gingerly examining the revolver Hack had given him for Christmas. She'd bet anything it was still where Semi had put it that night.

In the closet, to hide it from Gayner.

She stalked to the open closet door and stretched to sight along the overhead shelf. The brown paper sack was all by itself there, pushed to the very rear, far beyond her reach. With the same purposeful stride, she emerged into the room and spun around, searching for something to stand on.

"I just want what's mine," Ralph pouted, continuing to manicure his nails with the unwieldy knife. "You women think you're better than men, know that? Sherry, she got so smart, she didn't have to do what I said anymore. Clean the house? Not if she didn't feel like it. Pack my lunch? Mend my socks? All the stuff wives are supposed to do? Forget it."

April went to the bureau, lifted out the empty top drawer, turned it upside down, carried it to the walk-in.

"She wouldn't even go to bed when I said," Ralph continuted to complain, "unless I whopped her sometimes."

April laid the drawer on the floor in front of the shelf and test-rocked it with her toe.

"I tell you, lady, my Sherry has just made my life miserable."

Biting her tongue, April felt her fury for this man as a fever in her face, a quivering in all her extremities. She planted one foot on her improvised step stool and, gripping the edge of the shelf, hauled herself up. The brown paper bag teased, a scant three inches from her straining fingers.

*   *   *

Semi noticed the dented Chevy, in need of paint, parked at the foot of The Shelter's driveway, but he had more personal things to think about at the time.

Was April going to send him packing before he could even unpack? Would she sic her grandfather on him, shotgun and all? He'd had a long, frustrating day, and he was afraid he was in for more of the same.

As his tires crunched around the corner of the house, he saw her little black car parked in the barnyard. The kitchen windows reflected light like one-way mirrors, not revealing who might be in there watching him brake the truck to a stop. While he listened to the cooling motor tick for a minute, no welcoming face came to the door, no shout of gladness rang across the yard.

He hefted his suitcase and set it down again before getting out of the pickup. No use carrying it in if he wasn't going to be invited to stay. He hunched his shoulders, his hands in his sheepskin-lined pockets, and walked toward the porch, feeling like a salesman expecting to have a door slammed in his face.

One drawer wasn't enough. April got down and went to get another from the bureau.

"You know what's wrong with the world?" Ralph was saying. "Women's lib. Giving females the notion they're as strong and smart and sensible as men."

"Yeah, I sure would like to be more like you," April said, pulling out the middle drawer and upending it on the bed. The clothes she'd left behind spilled out.

Fleetingly pleased with herself that the superstition had worked again and here she was at The Shelter, she carried the drawer into the closet, stacked it on the first drawer, and cautiously stepped up.

The wood under her shoe popped ominously. Snatching

up the brown sack, she jumped off the makeshift stool and knelt, keeping her back to the room.

Ralph was warming to his lecture. "No way can Sherry make it without me. No way. You want to know why?"

Ripping open the bag, nearly scattering the handful of loose bullets, April noticed for the first time that Hack had glued a Santa sticker to the ugly black barrel. Impatient with her uncooperative, unsteady hands, she snapped open the cylinder and fed it full of bullets.

"See, Sherry's got to have a lot of supervision. She's not the smartest woman in the world."

"She's smart enough to leave you," April muttered. Pausing to consider, she removed the bullet from the first chamber and stuck it in her pocket.

"Oh, I admit I'm too hard on her sometimes, but she knows whatever I do is for her own good."

Holding the gun in both hands, April checked over her shoulder. Ralph was smiling at his manicure, rambling on about Sherry as if she were a dog he was putting through obedience school. April's eyes blurred and the revolver made her arms tremble. Ralph's voice, droning on and on, was her father's voice. The same self-satisfied tone. The same misogynistic philosophy.

Staring at the gun, heavy in her hands, she tried to hear Semi saying these carelessly cruel words. Never. He would never even *think* them; he'd be more disgusted and outraged to hear them than she was.

It was as if a flashbulb illuminated her store of muddled hopes and fears. For one sharp second, she saw that Semi was, despite his size and sex, more vulnerable than she.

Shaking her head to scatter distractions, she turned, still in a crouch, arms extended, gun aimed, mouth in a determined line. "Now get out. Now. Get. Out."

Ralph glanced up without much interest. His eyes

sharpened on the gun. "Does that shoot caps or water?"

"Bullets, dang it!" April jerked it from one target to another—his head, his midsection, his knees, his shoulder—aghast at the idea of putting a bullet in any part of him. "Don't be dumb," she both warned and pleaded.

"Show me."

"Show you!"

He folded his arms. "Damn right."

Damn idiot!

She stood up fully, aimed at the ceiling, and pulled the trigger on the empty chamber. In the ensuing quiet, the Santa sticker peeled free and floated to the floor.

"Here, let's see. You probably got the safety on," he said, standing, pocketing his knife.

"No! Stay there," she ordered, resisting the urge to enlighten him on revolvers and safeties. He wouldn't have listened to her anyway—he hadn't listened to the demand that he stand still.

"See, here's an example of what I was telling you," Ralph said as he walked at her. His hand reached out, fingers wriggling. "Where a woman messes up doing a man's job."

Lunging away from his grab at her, April hit the wall. Her finger flexed, the gun roared, and powdery ceiling plaster snowed over Ralph, freezing the disdainful sneer on his face.

"I want you out of here now," she panted, bringing the muzzle down to point it, again, at his assorted parts.

"Hey, listen, I can take a hint." He raised his hands in surrender and began a bobbing, backward retreat toward the hall door.

The stairs rattled with someone coming up fast, and as Ralph turned around in the doorway, Semi exploded through it. Clutching each other, they fell and rolled across the floor, grunting and muttering expletives, till they washed up against April's legs, pinning her to the wall.

"Stop it!" April yelled at the two men, who were trying to establish choke holds on one another.

Aiming once more at the ceiling, she fired another shot. This one loosened a square-foot chunk that thudded, unnoticed, inches from the pugilists' shoulders. The two continued to rabbit-punch and gouge each other.

Until Ralph pulled his knife.

The moment she realized why he'd let go of Semi's hair to jam that hand into the pocket of his camouflage pants, April knew it was time to stop pussyfooting around. Reversing the gun in her hand, squinting with distaste, she swatted at Ralph's upraised wrist. And missed.

The butt of the gun whizzed past his hand and rapped Ralph smartly above the right ear. April squeaked one surprised, dismayed monosyllable as the knife clattered to the floor and Ralph went limp, still embracing Semi.

Crawling out from under, gasping for breath, Semi took the hand April offered and stumbled upright.

"Are you okay?" they asked together, clutching each other's shoulders.

Semi gave April a quick hug, then bent to Ralph to check for a pulse. "Steady as she goes," he decided.

"Thank goodness. What are you doing here?" she asked ungraciously.

"I heard the shot as I came up on the back porch."

"No, I mean *here*. At all."

"I thought you might need some help fighting the bad guys. Looks like I was right."

"I was doing fine till you came through the door. He was on his way out, no problem, and then you jumped him, and now he'll probably sue me for the headache he's going to have when he wakes up.''

"You mean you weren't a damsel in distress? I'm not your hero?'' He glumly paced the room, trying to smooth down his scrambled hair. "No, of course not. You don't like fights; you could maybe admire me as a wimp, but now the truth is out. I'm not yellow, just sort of jaundiced.''

April ignored him, preoccupied with stirring through the jumbled clothes she'd dumped out of the bureau drawer. She was hunting for something suitable for tying Ralph up.

"Where's Hack?'' Semi asked.

"Outside, I guess.'' She picked out an old, shiny black bra and, kneeling beside Ralph, began to truss his hands with it.

"Who is this guy?'' Semi squatted beside her to oversee her knots.

"Sherry's husband.''

"Where's Sherry?''

"Beats me.'' She half stood and stretched across the bed to snag a pair of white lace panties to use around Ralph's ankles.

"Why wouldn't you wait for me to come with you?'' Semi put his forefinger on the filmy knot to help April draw it tight.

She tucked the loose ends neatly out of sight in the tops of Ralph's socks. "Because you were at work and I'm perfectly capable of handling my own affairs.''

"April.'' He grabbed her and pulled her into an awkward embrace leaning over Ralph's body. "You wouldn't let me come with you because you're afraid of me.''

"That's ridicul—''

"Yes, you are. At first you were afraid of me because you were afraid of men, period. But now you're

scared of me because of what I've done to your or-
derly little world. I've made you feel vulnerable and
dependent. Because that's what love does to people—
entangles them. And then it intensifies every feeling,
including pain.''

She shook her head, struggling to free herself. ''No
matter what you say—''

''I say you love me.''

''No,'' she wailed. ''I don't want to love you! Oh,
Semi, why do I love you?''

His grim expression softened as the words echoed in
their ears. She slumped, and gratefully she let him draw
her sideways around Ralph, so they could embrace
unencumbered.

''It's okay, sweetie,'' he soothed, stroking her back.
''Come on, give up and say you'll marry me.''

''Semi—''

''I'll let you be your own woman.''

''Semi—''

''You can write it right into the wedding vows. 'I,
April Lynn Parish, do not promise to honor or obey or
even be tactful—' ''

''April! What the hell's going on in here?'' Hack
bellowed from the doorway, making everyone except
Ralph leap to attention.

NINE

Hack's square shoulders filled the door. His shotgun dangled from one gnarled hand. He glared first at Semi, and his disposition didn't improve when he studied the recumbent, still unconscious Ralph.

"Who in blazes is that?"

"Sherry's husband," April said.

"Well, I'll be—" Hack stepped closer and squinted down at their prisoner. "It sure is. Gosh dang it. How the hell did he know to come here?"

"He said he followed Nora out. Is Sherry here?"

"No. Gone and won't be back."

"That's what I told him!" she said, as indignant as if she'd known all along that she was telling Ralph the truth.

"What's wrong with him besides mortification?" Hack asked.

"Mortification?"

"To be wearing ladies' undies."

"I gave him just a little tap on the head," April confessed. "Nothing else seemed to distract him from throttling Semi."

"Trying to throttle," Semi corrected her.

"Who the heck is that?" Patsy's voice was a fair imitation of Hack's. She was hopping up and down to see past his elbow into the room.

"Ralph Gr—" April began.

"Who the hell do we have here?" another voice exclaimed, and Hack stepped back to let Ivan through.

Squatting to thumb open Ralph's eyes one at a time, Ivan said, "Ralph Wilmer Greene. Damn, damn, damn. How did he come to be here?"

"Followed Sherry's sister out," Hack said. "We fell down there, sure enough."

Once again a newcomer loomed in the doorway and started to say, "Who—"

"Ralph Greene. He followed Nora here," April snapped, and then touched her hand to her mouth, seeing it was Clint. Knowing he was a gangster was a lot more intimidating than suspecting he was one.

Casually dropping his arm over April's shoulders, Semi said, "April and I can drive him to a doctor."

"Ivan can handle it," Hack said.

"Yeah, I'll take care of him. You want to give me a hand, Clint? Phew-ee! This guy smells worse than a wet dog."

"Uhh, Hack, I don't think we should let them take him—that is, give them the chance—I mean the *bother*—of dealing—" April drew in a deep breath, ready to try again.

"Nonsense." Hack cradled the shotgun and watched Ivan and Clint haul Ralph to his feet. "This is right up Ivan's alley, this line of work."

"That's what I mean," April pleaded in a carrying whisper. "Ralph doesn't stand a chance."

"What kind of chance did he give Sherry, eh?" Hack turned to follow the stumbling trio into the hall. Patsy had already disappeared.

April grabbed Semi's hand and shouted at her grandfather to wait. "We need to talk."

Hack shuffled his feet like a schoolboy afraid of missing recess. "Can't we do it later?"

"Now. Please. Now, Grandfather."

Sighing, he watched his boarders amble out of sight toward the front of the house before he returned to the room and closed the door. He motioned to the bed, and they all sat down on the edge like birds on a telephone wire.

"You two married yet?" Hack said as he stowed the shotgun on the floor under the bed, crossed his bony knees, and clasped his hands over them.

"No. Listen, Grandfather, you can't leave Ralph with those two goons. They'll certainly rough him up. They might even kill him." April's voice rose as her grandfather's head began to shake. "They're criminals, Hack. Clint's got some connection with the Mafia."

His head circled from negative to positive. "Well, you finally got something right. Clint has, indeed, been involved in organized crime."

April bounced closer to Hack, laying an earnest hand on his arm. "We've got to call the police."

Hack stared past her at Semi. "Sherry's husband's a hotheaded hotshot who beat her before, during, and after her pregnancy. She was staying here—hiding out—till the divorce was official, and now her sister's taken her to another part of the country to start fresh."

April said, "What's Sherry's relationship to Ivan and Clint?"

Hack's expression told her she'd asked something dumb. "None. Whatsoever."

"Well, then," she faltered, "how did Ivan recognize Ralph?"

"Had his picture. I did, too. So we'd know who to watch out for."

"You had others to watch out for, too," Semi said quietly.

April opened her mouth and snapped it shut again. Feeling as if the proverbial light bulb had just come on above her head, she said, "The Shelter is a shelter. For witnesses and victims in need of protection."

Hack was nodding at Semi. "We don't have photos of everyone who might be a threat. We have to be suspicious of any stranger. That's why I didn't take to you at first, Ruby."

"Oh, Hack," April chided. "You never take to anyone at first. Or seconds, or thirds, or—"

"That's why I'm good at this." Hack actually laughed. "I already got a reputation for being a loner and a terror. I can patrol my grounds daily and nobody notices. Inside is mostly Ivan's responsibility."

"But what about his counterfeit money?" April said.

"He's a Secret Service trainee. Studying all kinds of stuff like that."

Slumping against Semi's solid body, April sighed her relief.

"Clint's an informant on his former mob," Hack went on, apparently enjoying himself now. "And we got a murder witness coming in the first of next week."

"How long have you been running a safe house?" Semi asked.

"A couple months, in all." Hack poked April's arm with a sharp forefinger and cackled. "I bet you thought I was planning a bank robbery."

"Something like that." She leaned forward and returned the poke. "And you didn't want me hanging around your precious safe house. That's why you've been acting so pigheaded and making such unreasonable, outrageous demands that I get married."

"You're calling *me* pigheaded and unreasonable?" The old man puffed up his chest and glared down his nose at her. "You're the one who swore off marriage before she even knew for sure what it was. That's like a little kid deciding he hates ice cream when he hasn't even tasted it."

April rolled her eyes. "A person can't just 'taste' marriage."

"No, but you sure as hell could approach the idea with a broader-opened mind."

"Hack—"

"What's wrong with this fella here? He seems smart enough—figured out the safe-house situation before you did, I wager. Not bad-looking. Strong. Usually in a good humor. Doesn't pick his nose in public."

"Hack!"

The bed jiggled as the old man stood up. Reaching under his feet to reclaim the shotgun, he said, "You two can stay as long as you want on the understanding that it's at your own risk. And I'm trusting you not to tell *anyone* about this shelter we're running."

"Don't worry, Mr. Jones," Semi said. "You have my promise and my admiration."

Hack nodded before he leaned to stage-whisper at April, "He's polite, too."

April rolled her eyes again.

Hack opened the door, paused, and turned back. "Separate bedrooms, April Lynn," he said sternly.

For a full minute after her grandfather's departure, April sat trying to remember what life had been like a month ago, before she'd climbed two flights of creaking wooden stairs to hire herself a husband.

Heaving one long, exaggerated sigh, she turned and looked into Semi's eyes. "I want to be bone of your bone, flesh of your flesh. Please. Marry me, Semi."

His sweet, slow smile grew, stretching his mouth, crinkling his eyes. "I don't know what to say. Could I have a minute to think about it?"

Laughing, she fell against him, and his arms came around her, too gentle to be a prison. "One minute, no more. Because if you come to your senses and say no, I'm going to rend my garments and gnash my teeth."

"I don't know about the gnashing part, but the rending sounds kind of interesting." Threading his fingers into her hair, he cupped her head to kiss her brow, nose, chin.

They coasted backward on the bed, and he dragged her over him like a blanket. The warmth of his mouth on hers spread fire through her body.

Breaking the kiss, he lipped against her cheek, "Okay, the minute's up. I've thought it over, and all systems are definitely go."

"Some systems are more go than others, I think," she said, bumping playfully against him.

"Why?"

"Surely I don't have to explain male anatomy to you."

"No, I mean why did you just ask me to marry you?"

She pulled back to smile into his eyes. "To quote a real romantic guy, 'I think I love you.' " She wriggled down, head on his chest, and sighed. "And because of Ralph."

"Ralph? You mean when you thought he was going to kill me, it shook you so badly that—"

"No. You weren't in any danger. You and I were too smart for him." She shut her eyes. "No, Ralph just made me see things more clearly. Ralph Greene is the kind of husband I was always afraid I'd get. He probably was charming as all get-out before Sherry said, 'I do,' and from then on it was all *him* telling *her*, 'You *will*.' But Ralph isn't a normal man. He's sick."

"He needs professional help," Semi agreed.

"So did my father. Instead of fearing him, I should have been pitying him." She raised her face to look Semi in the eye again. "You aren't Ralph. You aren't my father."

"Thank my lucky stars," he whispered.

"You and I won't fight," she promised. "Not about anything important, anyway."

Hugging her to him, he rolled them both off the bed and pranced her around the room in a galloping waltz. "Semi's getting married in the morning," he sang breathily and off-key.

"No, no!" She stopped him with both hands on his chest and both boots on top of his. "Not in the morning. Hack won't let us sleep together tonight if we don't have the ceremony today. Now that I've made up my mind, I can't wait! I couldn't sleep another night without you in the bed."

Pretending to stroke luxuriant mustaches, Semi bragged, "You couldn't sleep *with* me in the bed, either."

April was discovering the meaning of "deliriously happy." The weight of indecision having lifted, she felt as if she were floating like a helium balloon, spinning like a whirligig.

"We have the license!" She anchored herself by throwing both arms around Semi's neck. "All we need is a minister."

"My brother-in-law is a Church of Christ minister," Semi said, clasping her to him with his hands molding the curves of her bottom.

"Dale's husband?"

"Right. As far as I know, he's in Dayton and could be here in a couple of hours—if he doesn't get as lost as I did."

"Your sister could come, too. And your mother. She'd want to see your wedding."

"I bet you didn't bring your wedding dress out here."

"What wedding dr—oh!"

"And I don't have my suit. Heck! And no rings. Or Flowers. Have you got something blue?"

"Don't make it complicated, Semi. Blue jeans will do. Come on."

She dragged him into the hall and they rattled down the back stairs.

Hack, Ivan, and Ralph Greene looked up at their noisy entrance into the kitchen.

Ralph was slumped in a chair, untied hands clasped in front of him on the barren tabletop. April winced to notice the welt above his ear, but she certainly wasn't going to apologize for having hit him. It was nothing compared with what he'd meant to do to Semi—or what he had done to Sherry.

Crossing to Hack, who stood, fists on hips, in the dining room doorway, April said, "Guess what. Semi and I are—no kidding—going to get hitched."

Hack fixed her with a skeptical stare.

"Honest. So is it okay if we invite a few people to the ceremony and have it in the front parlor? Like—tonight?"

Frowning across at Semi, Hack said, "What kind of scam is she up to now, son?"

"If it's ivory lies again, she sure has got me fooled," Semi admitted.

April nudged her grandfather in the ribs with an insistent elbow. "You'd better say yes before the magic potion Semi drank wears off."

This time Hack looked to Ivan, sitting across from Ralph, and raised his eyebrows.

"I don't see any problem," Ivan said. He turned to Semi and reached out to shake his hand. "Congratulations, Mr. Ruby."

April lifted the telephone receiver and offered it to Semi, who tucked it into his neck so that he could dial while digging a five-dollar bill out of his jeans. "Give this to Hack. For the long-distance bill."

"It won't be that much," she said.

"Hello, this is Semi. Who's this? Werewolf who? Could I talk to the den mother? No, I want to talk to Dale, good buddy." Covering the receiver with a palm, he said, "A fiver may not cover it, time we get through the chain of command."

"Well, Hack doesn't want your money," she began, saw Hack's expression, and hastily handed the bill to him.

Ralph heaved a heavy sigh.

"Hey," April said, eyes widening, "you said you cut the phone line."

Shrugging, he slumped lower. "So I lied."

"I bet it's not the first time either," she scolded. But she was thankful the telephone was in order.

"Dale?" Semi said. "Oh, Jo. Where's Dale? Yes, it's important enough to bother her, even there. But I'll settle for William. William. William! Okay, I'll wait."

"Big mistake, man," Ralph warned. "Marriage is a big mistake."

"William? No? Who—Gayner, would you please get Dale or William on this line right—" Semi leaned against the cupboard and winked reassuringly at April.

She said, "Ask for your mother. Maybe she's there."

He shook off the suggestion. "She's worse than the kids about getting a message straight. Oh, hi, Mom."

Smothering a laugh, April went to the sink for a glass of water.

"Well, let's be on our way, Greene," Ivan said, shrugging into his parka. "I'll be back in an hour or so, Hack." He grabbed the back of Ralph's chair to prevent it from capsizing during Ralph's abrupt push-off, and the two men tramped out.

While Semi continued to explain matters to his mother, April finished making the coffee she'd started more than an hour earlier. Taking down cups and saucers from the overhead cabinet, she said, "Shouldn't we have heard Ivan's car leave the barn by now?" She strolled to the back door to look into the yard.

Hack said, "They're walking to the road to Greene's car. Ivan'll get a lift back from the sheriff's office."

"Is it safe for Ivan to transport Ralph like that? He wasn't even wearing handcuffs."

"The fellow's a fool."

April didn't think Hack meant Ivan. "And you're acting as Clint's bodyguard in the meantime. Ralph didn't see him, did he?"

Hack's pursed lips expressed his disgust that she'd think them such gross amateurs.

The telephone receiver clattered onto its cradle, and Semi groaned. "I think Mom thinks I've committed some horrible crime."

"What? Doesn't she understand we're being married?"

"Yeah. She thinks it's because a wife can't testify against her husband."

Laughing, April went to comfort him with a hug. "What crime does she think you're capable of?"

"None," he said, his face glum, but his body joyous with the pressure of her against him. "That's why the police are on to me. I screwed up."

Peeping under her arm to be sure she'd heard Hack leaving on his appointed rounds, April purred to her husband-to-be, "You certainly did. And I have every reason to hope you shall again."

They took April's car back to Dayton, Semi driving, April pretending to doze with her head on his shoulder. Actually, she was considering how men like Ralph make marriage into a trap and men like Semi make it an inviting shelter.

On the outskirts of Dayton, April said, "Let's go to my place first. In fact, why don't you drop me there, and I'll shower and get dressed, and you can come back for me when you're ready?"

"Take your time. It'll be a while before I get everyone herded into William's van."

"You aren't going to bring all the kids!" she exclaimed.

"I'm not?" Then he relented and reassured her. "I'm not. But can I bring Gayner?"

"Yes, we need Gayner. He can be your best man. Best boy." Even while she was nodding, she said, "Oh, no. It's snowing. What if we can't get back to the farm tonight?"

"It's not going to snow that hard yet. What you have to worry about is all my relatives being snowbound at The Shelter for a couple of days."

They moaned in harmony.

The snow was a false alarm. At five o'clock, when April opened the blinds at her bedroom window to scout the street below, a pale moon glowed through the gray haze of smog and fog.

She checked herself in the full-length mirror for the dozenth time, pleased with the fit of the bright-flowered dress. Below the swirl of skirt, her cream stockings and shoes looked like spring. Pearl earrings and the gold chain bracelet Semi had given her for Christmas. Nothing on her shining hair. Almost new white slip. Gardenia perfume. Deodorant. Teeth brushed twice.

She perched on the edge of the couch, hands clasped, feeling like a bride—jittery and having second thoughts.

* * *

Semi was sweating into his new gray suit, standing by his mother's elbow while she smeared peanut butter on bread. Gayner swayed before the open refrigerator, snapping his fingers, taking stock of the pop supply.

"It's only a two-hour trip, Mom. Snacks on the way aren't necessary."

"Better safe than sorry," she said, shoving her camel coat sleeves higher before dipping knife into jar again.

"Yeah, that Patsy's cooking sure ain't worth waiting for," Gayner said, swaggering to the counter with a six-pack of root beer.

Dale swept into the room, a navy blue tornado, still trying to attach obstinate earrings. "Gayner, don't you have anything but tennies to wear?"

"Uh-huh. Bedroom slippers."

"Do they look better than the tennies?"

William came into the room and sat down to tie his respectable black shoes. His black flannel suit, blue-striped shirt, string tie, and navy suspenders, along with his salt-and-pepper beard, gave him the air of a Victorian preacher on his way to a revival meeting.

"I must write a poem for you and this wonderful occasion," Wanda said. " 'Now bring they love in fullest hearts. Ta-tum, ta-tum, ta-tum, ta-parts!' "

She began wrapping the sandwiches as if they were made of glass, slowly and with infinite care. Having completed one, she sighed and shook it open to try again.

"Mom, let me help," Semi offered, casting a despairing glance at the wall clock.

"I can manage. I'm sure you have things to do," she said.

"I do, I do!"

Hearing her brother's tone, Dale stepped in to finish the job with her usual efficiency. "Go warm up the van, William. We're on our way."

"I gotta use the bathroom," Gayner announced and rushed out.

"That's a good idea," Wanda said, beginning to stroll purposefully after him.

William cracked the backdoor open, shivered once, and looked over his shoulder at Dale. "Do I have a coat around here someplace?"

"Try the front closet," she said. "Oh, the camera!" She shoved the sandwiches at Semi and whirled out of the room.

Semi shut his eyes and sank onto a kitchen stool. He felt like a butterfly collector with a net full of holes.

For all he knew, right this minute, his prize butterfly, having had time alone to think, might be deciding to make a break for it herself!

Buck had picked up Dusty just before dusk. Now the dark sedan steadily chewed the miles between Cincinnati and the yellow highlighted spot on the map.

"I sure hope Clint didn't louse up these directions. All I need is to spend the night driving in circles out in the boondocks," Dusty grumbled.

Buck grunted agreement.

The two men continued to make infrequent, lethargic remarks about the weather, families, and sports till Dusty readjusted the holster under his left arm and settled down to sleep.

First April had switched on the TV and perched on the edge of the sofa. Next she had made a cup of instant coffee. Now she kicked off her shoes and lounged, cup in one hand and stale doughnut in the other, watching a film about salmon fishing.

She wasn't worried or angry—Semi had warned her that it would take a while to round up his family.

When the telephone rang, she expected it to be him, calling to say they were on their way at last.

Instead, Hack's gruff voice demanded without preamble, "Semi there with you?"

What was this, a test? A surprise bed check?

"No," she answered tartly. "He's at his house, getting ready for his shotgun wedding."

"What's the phone number?"

"What do you want to know for?" she asked suspiciously.

"Did you two happen to see Ivan Como anywhere on the road on your way back to the city?"

Surprised, she had to rearrange her thoughts to come up with the correct answer. "No. Has something happened?"

"What's Semi Ruby's number?"

"Hack! I'm kin. Will you please talk to me?"

"I *am* talking to you, April Lynn! I'm saying, 'Give me the goddamn number!' "

Defeated, knowing the next thing he'd do if she persisted would be to slam down the receiver, April recited Semi's phone number. "But, Hack—"

There was a crash, but it wasn't the telephone being disconnected. Her grandfather's raspy breathing continued to sound in her ear.

"What was that?" she demanded, just as a second bang reverberated along the phone line. This time there was also the unmistakable clattering rain of breaking glass. "Hack!"

"Gotta go," he said in his normal, stoic way. Click. Dial tone.

Semi's tap on the horn was only a warning; as soon as he'd done it, he rolled out of the Honda and sprinted upstairs to escort April. After pounding on the apartment door, he jogged nervously in place.

Just as he raised his fist to knock again, the door swung open, and he teetered eye to eye with this beautiful woman he was about to marry. Wide, solemn, dark eyes, she had. Right now they bored into him like a drill sergeant's.

Then she smiled, the slow, welcoming smile of a woman for a man, and he wanted to sweep her ahead of him into the bedroom, tear off the perfect dress, forget the van full of expectant relatives waiting below, make love to her now and all night.

Her first words confused him, breaking the spell. "What did he want?"

"What did who want?"

"Didn't Hack call you?" Her expression changed to one of worry. "Oh, God! I tried to call him back and his line was busy, so then I tried to call you and your line was busy, so I thought you were talking to each other." She was bustling toward the telephone as she spoke.

Semi shrugged, not sure why she was upset. "There're ten kids at my house. The phone's always busy."

She lifted the receiver and stabbed out Hack's number. "He wanted to know how to reach you and asked if we'd seen Ivan, and then there were these loud crashes and he said he had to go."

Before she could accelerate her worry up to cruising speed, Hack answered the phone with a curt "What?"

" 'What' is right," April said. "What's going on out there? What were those crashes I heard?"

"Is Semi Ruby with you now?"

"Yes, but—"

"Put him on."

Raising her arms in a disgusted gesture of defeat, April pointed the receiver at Semi, who shrugged out of his overcoat as he strode across the room to take it. April snuggled up to him, forcing his free arm around her, resting her head against his neck. It felt great, but mostly she did it in hopes of hearing both sides of the conversation.

"This is Semi."

"I could use your help tonight, son." Hack's words were faint, but distinct to April.

"Certainly. What—"

"Have you got a dog?"

"A—no, I don't."

"Well, that's okay. I don't like dogs anyway. But I could use you."

"Just tell me what—"

"Ivan's disappeared. I need myself a deputy for the night."

"Shouldn't the police—"

"I can explain it all when you get here. Come alone."

April jerked back her head, but Semi muffled her protest by spreading his hand over her mouth.

"But, sir, it'll take me two hours to get there. I still think the police—"

"If you don't stop gabbing, it'll take way more than two hours. Are you coming or not?"

"Yes, sure, if—"

Hack had hung up without signing off.

Rushing to pick up her coat and purse, April backtracked to shut off lamps, muttering to herself. "First he insists I get married, and then he snatches the groom away before the ceremony. This better be a real emergency. He better have a damned good excuse for—"

Semi grabbed her around the waist, bringing her to a full stop against his hip. "Where do you think you're going? Hack said I should come alone."

"He meant no wedding guests," she said, squirming to free herself and only succeeding in tightening his grip.

"If it's dangerous, I don't want you there."

"If it's dangerous, I don't want *you* there," she echoed. "You don't even know how to shoot a gun."

"I don't need to know how, because I wouldn't want to hurt anyone."

Love for this man eddied through her, making her stretch forward to taste the strong curve of his lower lip.

Relaxing his hold into a cherishing embrace, Semi bent his face to meet hers. Hack, Ivan, and the waiting wedding party evaporated in the heat of the kiss.

Then, reluctantly, Semi twisted his mouth free and forced himself to let her go. "Stay here, love," he said quietly, without expectation that she'd listen.

"This is your big chance." She stepped back two paces and, folding her arms, watched him with amusement. "You've been swearing up and down how you'll let me be me. How marriage won't make any difference in my independence." Swinging her purse onto her shoulder, she gave him a broad wink. "I'm going with you. What do you say to that?"

"I say—" He picked up his coat, shaking his head in rueful bafflement. "Fools rush in where smart, prudent, *easy-to-get-along-with* women fear to tread."

TEN

Now and then a kamikaze snowflake found their windshield, but the moon still rode through the clouds as the Honda hummed northward, Semi driving.

They had dismissed the wedding guests with profuse apologies and promises that it was only a rain check, not a change of heart. Semi's mother was especially sympathetic, if not understanding. She advised April to write to Ann Landers for help with their differences, adding that she should use aliases to protect their privacy because "Swinburne isn't a common name, you know."

April, having decided not to waste the next two hours worrying about what was going on at The Shelter, wriggled into a more comfortable slump against Semi's shoulder and shut her eyes in hope of sleep.

"I'm glad I hired you," she said, having given sleep at least a thirty seconds' chance.

"Me, too. Even if you did stiff me for the paycheck."

"I think it kept slipping my mind because, as long as I owed it to you, there'd still be a tie between us."

"I'm sure the collection agency I hired will appreciate that excuse. It's so much more creative than 'The check is in the mail.' "

She traced a happy face on his kneecap. "If you sic a collection agency on me, I won't give you a good reference for your résumé."

"Oh? What good things would you have said about me?"

" 'This man is dependable and hard.' Hard-working, I mean," she said, laughing as he pinched her ribs. "But you won't need a résumé unless you're changing jobs."

"I don't see myself working at the employment office the rest of my life."

"Okay, but *I* don't see you working as a surrogate husband the rest of your life." Still tracing circles on his leg, her hand drifted higher. Higher. "In fact, if I catch you moonlighting, I will cut off all your fringe benefits."

Semi's shudder wasn't one hundred percent fake.

April surprised herself by actually falling asleep. Even more surprising, Semi found all the correct back roads' turns to get them to the farm. It was the rutted lane that shook her awake.

The sight of the dark, unwelcoming house brought all her worries flooding back. "Do you think Ralph Greene's responsible for Ivan disappearing?"

"Possibly."

"If we should need your revolver, it's back on the closet shelf where I found it," she advised him bleakly.

Semi squeezed her knee.

They rounded the corner into the backyard. The kitchen lights were dim as lanterns in a cave. Coasting to a stop and killing the headlights, Semi ducked his head to look past April at the porch. Something seemed different about it.

"Oh, God," April whispered. "The backdoor's boarded up."

Squinting, Semi saw what she meant. Not over the entire doorway, but where there should have been a glass pane, an oversized, badly warped sheet of plywood had been nailed up.

"Stay here a minute," Semi said, opening the door. As soon as April swung her legs sideways, ready to open her door, he said more insistently, "I'm not commanding you, I'm asking you. Let me be a little independent, too."

An insight streaked through April's mind—a vision of herself as an elderly, nagging, overbearing wife. Meekly she leaned back against the seat.

"Be careful," she said.

Too preoccupied to appreciate this small victory, Semi crossed the yard. His heart was beating as if he'd just finished a half hour's run. His shoes crunched on the frosty grass and creaked on the porch step.

"Hack?" he called softly, rapping on the rough plywood patch.

The door swung inward, and Hack's gangling silhouette stretched a monstrous shadow across the floorboards. He motioned to Semi to hurry in.

Semi turned toward the Honda and repeated the motion, and Hack snorted his disgust. "Didn't I tell you to come alone?"

April raced across the open space, jumped onto the porch, and ducked under her grandfather's arm supporting the door. "I stowed away," she panted.

The kitchen smelled of coffee and cats. A fire in the fireplace snapped and swirled. Stripping off her coat, April went to the stove, hefted the coffeepot, and overturned two cups from the dish drainer.

Pouring, she said, "How'd the glass get broken?"

Hack eased himself into his favorite chair at the table

and, as usual, ignored her question to ask one of his own. "Did you happen to see Patsy on your way here?"

"Now Patsy's missing, too?' April exclaimed.

Taking one of the cups, Semi sat down across from Hack.

"Did I say she was missing?" The old man smacked the table, making Semi's coffee slop over the side. "No. Can you believe it? She quit on me. Without any notice."

"Hack, she's been telling you she was quitting every day since you hired her."

"Exactly," Hack said, and jutted his jaw with a clicking of false teeth.

This did seem to make a weird sort of sense, Semi thought as he worked a chair out and nudged April to sit in it. "Did she give a reason for really leaving this time?"

Hack grunted. "Said shooting made her nervous."

"Someone shot the door out?" April cried, twisting around to peer at it again.

"No, no. Patsy did that herself. Slammed it one too many times when she was stomping in and out carrying her things to the porch."

Glancing sidelong at April, noticing she was about to explode with impatience, Semi interceded. "Sir, please, would you tell us the whole story from when we left for Dayton this afternoon?"

The reasonable appeal made Hack stroke his chin in contemplation. Into the quiet, a kitten mewed from below the table, and Hack wasted another minute fumbling around his feet to pick her up.

Massaging the handful of gray fur, he said, "First thing that happened was nothing happened."

April opened her mouth, and Semi gently but firmly laid a finger across her lips.

"Ivan had said he'd be back in an hour. He didn't come back and he didn't come back. It started to get dark, and I figured he must have had car trouble. But then why didn't he call me and say so?"

Sipping at his coffee, Semi nodded. April put her chin on her hand in an attitude of attention. The kitten's purring was noisy and steady as an alarm clock's buzz.

"Well, I've got Clint to watch out for, and I never had to do it all on my own before. To do it right takes two. So I says to Patsy, did she know how to handle a gun, because she was going to have to patrol instead of wash dishes tonight. And that's when she got all huffy and hostile and door-happy."

Semi hated to interrupt Hack's narrative, but he had to ask, "Where's Clint now, sir?"

"Gone."

"Gone!" April's bellow frightened the kitten into a broad jump from Hack's lap to a chair four feet away. "You mean you cheated me out of my wedding, my wedding *night*, by begging my groom to come out to these boondocks—come alone, you told him—to guard some good-for-nothing crook—" Here she shook Semi's placating hand off her arm. "—and the bastard isn't even here for anyone to guard?"

Hack stared at her for a moment before his rare grin appeared. "That's about the size of it."

The old man settled himself, one arm draped on the chair back, and addressed April's complaint. "See, at the time we spoke on the telephone, I didn't know Clint was going to be gone tonight. When I did find out, you were on your way."

"Okay," she conceded. "Go on."

"Not much left to tell. I finally got a call from Ivan. Halfway to the interstate, Greene's clunker car clunked its last. When Ivan put his head under the hood to see what the trouble was, Greene slammed it down on him.''

"I *told* you he shouldn't transport Ralph that way," April interjected.

"When Ivan came to, he was lying in the side ditch, Greene and the car had gone, and it was going on six o'clock. By the time he flagged down a ride and got his head seen to and phoned me, it was another hour gone. Too late for me to wave you off.''

April frowned into her coffee cup. "So Patsy left just before we got here? She wasn't walking, was she?" she asked, prepared to be outraged anew.

"You sure you didn't pass her on the lane up? Ivan was driving her.''

"Ivan—he got back?''

"Sheriff dropped him off. Patsy was so het up about leaving, Ivan said he'd take her to the nearest bus stop. In spite of his headache.''

"And Clint is—''

"Went along for the ride. He was out of cigarettes.''

"Is that safe? For him to be out in public?''

"He's rode along with Ivan before after dark. He stays in the car.''

April dropped back in her chair, mirroring Hack's relaxed pose. "So now what? We turn around and waste another two hours driving back to Dayton?" The thought of spending the night here in a big, cold bed by herself made the corners of her mouth roll down.

Semi tipped onto one hip to dig out the wallet from his rear pocket. Extracting a five, he offered it across the table to Hack. "May I use your phone?''

Hack reached toward the bill, drew back his hand, and wiped the palm across his mouth. "This time it's on the house.''

"Who're you going to call?" April asked Semi's back as he stood at the counter dialing.

"It's only nine-thirty." He turned around and settled on his heels to wait. "The line isn't as busy after nine," he added before saying into the receiver, "Hi, Dale? Great. Is everyone still dressed? Good. How would you feel about driving up here for a midnight wedding ceremony?"

April tapped the side of her empty cup with a fingernail, excited that the off-again marriage might be on-again. Most families would decline the invitation at this late hour. She was betting Semi's family would be there with bells on.

"Here's April to give you directions." Semi held out the receiver, and she sideswiped the table with a hip, hurrying to accept it.

"Didn't we go by this corner once before already?"

"Shut up. If we did, it's because I can't concentrate when you're all the time yapping."

"All these country roads look alike."

"What's your hurry? Clint's not going anywhere."

"Ho, boy, you sure got that right." Buck's laugh rumbled like the wooden bridge they'd just crossed.

The headlights of a car swept across the barnyard. April, who'd been washing dishes near a window, announced it to the men.

Hack picked up the shotgun and went to peer into the yard. "Sounds like Ivan. Yep, there he goes into the barn."

Semi set aside the newspaper crossword puzzle he'd been working on and stretched, peering at his wristwatch in the process. Eleven-three.

Hanging the gun in its rack, the old man cracked open the porch door and waited till he could see the whites of Ivan's eyes before swinging it wide.

Clint came into the kitchen first, cupping a hand to

his face to light a fresh cigarette. Ivan brought up the rear. Patsy clumped along between them.

Hack snorted to see her. "Speaking of bad pennies—"

"Don't you start with me," she said, shaking her mittened fist under his nose. "I can change my mind if I want." She squinted belligerently at April.

"Hey, I think it's great you haven't left after all," April said. "Hack does, too, but he won't admit it. Why would he want to have to go through the rigmarole of hiring someone new? I'd hit him up for a raise right away, if I were you."

Ignoring them both, Hack said to Ivan, "Is anything wrong?"

"Naw. We missed the last bus, is all. While she was trying to decide whether to spend the night in the station, a wino asked her to buy him a lottery ticket, and a guy in a white fur coat suggested she join his stable."

"What do I know about horses?" she said, throwing off her coat as if it were a wrestling opponent. "Here, don't use a scouring pad on that skillet; you'll scratch it." And she shooed April away from the sink, drawing on her rubber gloves with a businesslike snap.

"Ms. Parish, Mr. Ruby." Ivan acknowledged them with nods. "Or is it Mrs. Ruby now?"

"Not yet," April said. "Soon. How's your head?"

He twisted his neck around to show her the fat, square bandage that swathed the back of his skull. "What hurt the worst was letting them shave off the hair."

Semi touched his own head and said, "I know what you mean."

"I'm going to bed," Clint announced, lumbering through the dining room doorway.

Wishing he could, too, Semi glanced at his watch again. Eleven-thirteen.

*　　*　　*

At eleven-twenty-eight, April suggested they go up-stairs and check out the accommodations.

"I got the blue room done," Patsy piped up. "Just in case."

"Just in case," Semi said, giving April a meaningful look. "That's our slogan."

The two of them trudged upstairs, April first and Semi's supportive hands on her waist. Turning on and shutting off lights in sequence as they made their way to the front south wing, they linked arms and leaned into each other.

"You know what would be fun?" she said. "To have a marathon up here some weekend, and make love in every room."

Pretending to stagger at the idea, he crowded her into the wall and snaked his chilly hands inside her coat to explore for bare skin, making April squeal and shimmy. When he would have settled into a real and tender kiss, she ducked free and pulled him along the hall.

"Last one there's a loser," she chortled and shook off his grip on her hand to pelt the last thirty feet, her heels as loud as flamenco taps.

Reaching through the open door, she switched on the overhead fixture.

Named for its navy-and-white floral wallpaper, the blue room was really mostly faded beige—rug, bed-spread, lace curtains, and upholstered furniture. The scent of Patsy's pine disinfectant lingered. The center-piece antique, a massive, intricately carved oak bed, sported white sheets and blankets invitingly turned down.

"Patsy even laid a fire for us," Semi said, walking toward the tile-and-marble fireplace.

While he sauntered around inspecting the room, April tried to see her husband-to-be as a stranger would see him. In spite of what Semi seemed to think, he wasn't overweight, but bone-and-muscle big. Not hand-some in the usual sense—his face was too openly cheru-bic to be that of a leading man—still he had an appeal, an attitude, a maleness, that was better than hand-someness. When he twisted around and smiled at her, her center stirred with reawakening desire.

He sat on the side of the bed, bouncing to test the mattress. Patting it beside him, he beckoned her.

"God, I wish we could just lie down and go to sleep right now," she said to cover her sudden, unaccount-able shyness. Walking across the few feet of threadbare carpet to him, she felt like a blushing schoolgirl on her first date.

Semi slipped his arm around her hips and drew her down. "I wish we could just lie down and *not* go to sleep right now."

She snickered.

He brushed the back of his hand lightly along her jaw. "I'm afraid to touch you, because if I start, I won't be able to stop."

Feeling boneless, April rested against him and fin-gered the gleaming blond highlight of hairs on his wrist. His shaved chin prickled against her cheek as he fas-tened his lips over hers, making desire, deep inside her, circle and begin to boil.

He lifted and lowered her to the bed. She lay on her back, limp as a rag doll, her glazed eyes appreciating how he filled out the gray trousers. He knelt over her, and his thigh was heavy and warm between her legs.

"You're beautiful," he murmured. "Gleaming. All of you a promise. I love you."

Something shifted inside her, and she let a tear trickle into her ear. "Independence is great, Semi Ruby, but sometimes it's a little scary. You're my safe house."

*   *   *

"See. On the upper floor," Dusty pointed out the light to Buck.

They were parked in the shadow of the woods, smoking and plotting.

"Yeah, I see it. But I don't see any other lights."

"Of course not. They're going to be under blackout conditions at night. You think we could just come out here and take potshots through the open windows?''"

"So where do you think Clint's at?''

"I don't know yet. Let's stroll around the grounds one time and get our bearings before we burst in and rescue him."

Both men laughed at the word "rescue."

Smiling at the ceiling, Semi stroked April's completely clothed back and admired their willpower, hers and his. They'd been here all of ten minutes without going to sleep or making mad, passionate love.

"I wish," he said, "that the first time I saw you standing in front of my desk, looking so grim and gorgeous, I could also have seen me putting my hand here"—she squirmed—"two weeks later. Is life amazing or what?"

"And I would never have believed two weeks ago that the quiet, rather sarcastic man behind that desk would make me so crazy I'd throw away all my good intentions about career and celibacy—"

"Lady, you never wanted to be celibate—"

"Listen, once the old body starts to go, a single woman doesn't have a lot of choice."

"Gosh, you think it's started to go yet?" he asked with mock concern, lifting aside her coat to survey the damage.

She punched his ribs, he tickled hers, and the mattress wheezed with their brief roughhouse.

"Shh." April sat bolt upright. "Is that a car coming up the lane?"

"Couldn't be." Semi straightened his arm over his head to once more consult his watch. "Well, maybe it could. If Dale was doing the driving."

"Let's go see." Grabbing the bedpost for leverage, she scrambled up, as excited as she'd ever been awaiting Santa Claus.

By the time April and Semi reached the kitchen, Dale, Wanda, William, and Gayner were in it, forming an ill-at-ease semicircle in front of the back door. Wanda had taken the time after arrival to collect the empty soda cans and sandwich wrappers from the van, and now she was committing these into Patsy's care.

Dale was saying, "What a wonderful painted lady you have here," and for an awful moment, April thought she meant Patsy.

"Built in 1870," Hack said, slipping his hands under his suspenders and rocking on his heels. "Cost a mint to build today."

Gayner was finding it necessary to tie and retie his sneaker laces, his face buried in his knee, till he heard Semi's welcoming voice.

"Hi, folks. Sorry to bring you out here so late. Have you all met each other yet?"

"We just walked in," Dale said, twisting around to smile at her husband, who was still jammed between the door and her back.

Taking a deep breath, concentrating on the etiquette of introductions she'd learned in home economics class, April said, "Mrs. Ruby, this is my grandfather, Hackett Jones. Hack, Semi's mother, Wanda Ruby." Then her mind went unmercifully blank.

With smooth aplomb, Semi came to the rescue. "And my sister, Dale Ritter. My brother-in-law, William—Reverend Ritter to his friends. And you remember Gayner." Peering around the room to see who had been left out, Semi continued. "This lady is Patsy, who is Hack's right and left hand. And these are some of his cats."

"I hadn't met William," April said, stretching her hand to shake his. "Thank you for helping us out on such meager notice."

The minister blinked and seemed for a moment to be trying to recall what it was he was doing for them. "Perhaps you and Semi would sit down with me to discuss the vows you want to make."

"Yes, of course."

Wanda rubbed her hands together briskly. "How about if I make us all some coffee?"

"Patsy, take everyone's coat," Hack commanded.

Wrapping hers tighter, Wanda wandered toward the range top. Everyone else stacked a garment onto Patsy's short arms, and she disappeared toward the dining room to, April suspected, lay her burden on the floor.

"Is there a piano?" Dale wondered. "I can play for the ceremony."

To April's surprise, Hack smiled and offered to show Dale the parlor. Gayner pranced off in their wake.

April lifted a cat off the nearest kitchen chair and sat down, William took a seat next to her, and Semi settled across the table.

Producing a *Book of Common Prayer* and a yellow legal pad, William said, "How much of the traditional love, honor, and obey ritual would you like to incorporate?"

Wanda began opening cupboard drawers and doors, ostensibly looking for coffee cups, but lingering and tch-tching over each disclosure. Patsy came back and began rooting in the refrigerator, mumbling about left-over ham.

"We can promise to honor," Semi said. "Even two

people who hate each other can honor each other. But obey is out. I don't expect my wife to take orders from me and vice versa.''

"Oh, yeah? You can't tell me not to put 'obey' in our vows," April joked.

Looking pained, William suggested, "What about love? 'I promise to love?' ''

"A person can't promise to love forever," April said. "That's a feeling, an involuntary reflex. Who knows how we'll feel about each other when we're ninety?''

His chin on his hand, one elbow planted on the table, Semi gave her a long, sad stare. He'd loosened his tie and collar, and his throat looked warm and inviting.

"I don't need to promise to love Semi," she elaborated softly. "That's as ridiculous as promising I'll eat and sleep.''

His face crinkled into a smile. Tapping the legal pad with a forefinger, he said, "Love's out. Obey's out. Honor goes without saying, so it might as well be out, too. Read us what we've got so far, William.''

The line between William's bushy eyebrows deepened. '' 'Dearly beloved.' '' He looked up expectantly. "Would you like to add anything else?''

'' 'Dearly beloved.' Yuck," April said. "That sounds like a funeral.''

"Strike 'dearly beloved,' '' Semi said.

William's sigh levitated the top sheet of the legal pad.

Wanda leaned over April's shoulder to look at the blank page. She smelled like lilies of the valley with just a dash of mothballs. "I should have brought some of my poetry books for you to quote out of. Do you remember any of the lines you used to recite for me, Swinburne?''

"How about Sir John Suckling?''

"Yes?" April waited expectantly.

" 'Out upon it! I have loved / three whole days together, / and am like to love three more— / if it prove fair weather.' "

April groaned. "Just say something in your own words, and I'll do the same."

"You mean ad-lib? What I feel? Like, my whole body's celebrating this happy occasion—my knees are clapping, my stomach's turning cartwheels—"

"You know what I mean," she scolded. "Go off in a corner for a few minutes and think of something good."

"Something that sounds good, or something I really mean?"

Shutting one eye, she compressed her mouth in mock anger. "Both, mister. If you want to live happily ever after."

Twisting sideways in the chair, his arm hooked over the back, Semi stared at the fireplace and tapped his thumbnail against his chin.

Dale and Hack came into the kitchen carrying on a one-sided, animated conversation about landmark designation of historical homes.

"Six fireplaces," Dale said. "Tin ceilings. Chandeliers. And the furniture! No wonder you love this place, April."

And she did love it. Even more so, now that it had indirectly brought her Semi.

On the outside, south of the porch, Dusty cut the telephone line, and Buck smacked a bullet ready in his .45 automatic.

ELEVEN

"There was one peanut butter sandwich left," Wanda said. "We could split it—let's see—eight ways."

April had helped herself to a page of the legal pad and jotted a few key words on it: "Sharing." "Faithful." "Teaching me to love." *Too sentimental*, she thought, scratching it all out and writing a frivolous "I'm yours—let's bed down!"

She glanced up guiltily, to see if anyone could have seen what she'd doodled. Semi had shut his eyes, presumably the better to think, but his deep breathing sounded suspiciously like snoring. Wanda, unable to find anyone else interested, was eating the peanut butter sandwich, one hand cocked on her hip, listening to Dale expound on original hardwood floors. Hack had settled in his chair by the fireplace, his wrists crossed on his crossed knees, a dangling foot swinging to some slow, inaudible music. William and Gayner leaned against a kitchen counter in twin poses—arms folded, chins tucked in, eyes glassy with boredom. Patsy was just coming down the back stairs apparently having gone up to collect her cleaning supplies; she clanked into the kitchen, fairly bristling with mops, brooms, buckets, and spray cans.

That was when the kitchen window nearest the fireplace burst into a thousand glittering pieces.

Semi stood up so fast his chair skidded backward and broadsided Patsy, sending her cleaning gear up and out in an explosion that rivaled the window's. William and Gayner had clutched each other convulsively, and immediately William reached out to draw Dale under his other wing. Wanda began to shuffle toward the broken glass, clucking her tongue, till Semi reached out and snagged her by the coat sleeve.

Hack, meanwhile, had leaped from the chair with impressive alacrity for an octogenarian and, his arms open wide, began herding everyone before him. "Into the dining room. Hurry. Move it. Semi, lock that porch door, Patsy, shut off the goddamn light."

Just before blackness plunged over them, April saw Hack stoop to pick something out of the window debris. Reaching into the dark where she'd last seen Wanda, April raised her voice above the general hubbub and scuffling of feet. "This way, Mrs. Ruby." A cold hand containing the remains of a sticky sandwich fumbled and grasped April's.

Someone stepped on a cat and the yowl triggered several human yelps. The confused, bumping, milling exodus seemed to take forever; it was long enough that April's eyes began to adjust to the dark. She could see Hack's outline by the gun rack, taking down his favorite shotgun. Semi's body loomed at her elbow to help her help his mother. They crowded into the pitch-black dining room, and Hack swung shut the adjoining door and threw a bolt before switching on the overhead light.

Everyone stood at odd angles around the antique trestle table, blinking, as if engaged in a game of statues. April looked first at the row of brocade-draped windows; shutters had been installed on the inside, new and raw without paint.

Shotgun on his shoulder, Hack marched to the opposite end of the room, threw open the hall door, and shouted, "Ivan!"

"What's going on here, Swinburne?" his mother said, drawing out a ladder-backed chair that was missing a few rungs. Sitting down, she absently finished the sandwich.

"I'm not completely sure. Hack will tell us in a minute."

Patsy brushed angrily at a smear of green cleanser on her white shirt. "I knew I shouldn't have stayed another day."

Ivan rocketed into the room, catching himself on the doorjamb to avoid colliding with Hack. He was wearing blue plaid pajamas, backless slippers, and his shoulder holster. It was the first time April had actually seen the gun he carried there. It was a long-barreled revolver that looked capable of knocking down—had she been shooting it earlier that day—not just plaster but the entire roof.

"Clint in his room?" Hack said.

"I'll check."

"Lock him in," Hack called as Ivan sprinted away. The old man motioned to April. "Hold this for me. Stay ready."

"This" was the shotgun. It felt heavy as a barbell, especially since she held it, pointing up, well away from her new, flowered dress.

Ivan skidded back. "What's going down?"

Displaying the rock he'd retrieved from the kitchen floor, Hack flicked it with one finger. "This was heaved through the kitchen window. Someone's probably crawling through after it right now."

"There's a note tied to it!" April exclaimed, dumbfounded that such a thing could happen anywhere but in old movies.

More precisely, the note had been rubber-banded. Hack worked it free, read to himself, handed the note to Ivan, who tilted it to the light and read, " 'Send out Clint and nobody gets hurt.' " Ivan snorted one cynical laugh. "No one except Clint."

"How in *the hell* did they find him?" Hack said.

"Who is Clint?" Dale stage-whispered to Semi.

"Is this one of those mystery weekends I've heard about?" Wanda asked, tucking her hands into her coat sleeves, Mandarin-style. "Where someone pretends to be murdered and we have to figure out who done it?"

"No, ma'am," Ivan said. "Folks, we have a danger-ous situation here, and Hack and I ask you to do exactly what we tell you when we tell you, so we all come out safe and sound."

For a moment no one spoke, and the room rustled with their quickened breathing.

Ivan continued. "You see, Hack has a safe house here for people to stay temporarily when they're in trou-ble. In Clint's case, he's an ex-mobster who's promised to testify against his former associates—some of whom are obviously outside right now."

April watched Semi's family absorb this news. They all seemed calm and resigned except for Gayner, whose eyes and body jittered with apparent, eager anticipation.

"I can slip back into the kitchen and phone for help," Semi offered.

Hack shook his head. "They'll have cut the line. Help couldn't get here fast enough anyhow."

"You won't send Clint out there, will you?" Dale wanted to know.

"No. Not even if we could trust them to go away peaceably if we did." Ivan waited for a moment to let the significance of the statement sink in.

"These men live by the sword and enjoy their work," Semi interpreted.

"Afraid so."

April spoke up. "But maybe we outnumber them. And we're bound to be smarter than they are. If they're anything like Clint," she couldn't help adding.

"Number means nothing," Ivan said. "All you civilians would be safer upstairs. Hack can find you a hiding place so that, no matter what the outcome, you'll be okay."

"April, you know the house," Hack said. "You take everyone and—"

"Gayner can take them," she said, and was rewarded with his suddenly military stance. "I know how to use a gun and I'm staying with you."

"I know how to use a gun, too," William said. "Vietnam."

"I know, too," Wanda said. "Tin cans in Daddy's pasture."

"I know," Gayner said, rushing to join the chorus. "My mom's boyfriend Lizard—"

"Okay, okay!" Ivan held up his hands for silence. "We're a regular army here. But I can't involve you. It's too dangerous."

"What about the second part of my theory?" April interjected. "That we have the drop on these thugs intelligence-wise?"

No one answered. The room's cold was beginning to seep into bones and numb thought, or so it seemed to April. She kept admonishing herself to *think*.

Abruptly, the hush and another kitchen window were broken. When the bang-clatter-tinkle died, a voice, muffled by distance and the closed dining room door, shouted, "Five minutes."

Hack touched a trembling hand to the top of his head. "We might save Clint's hide in a shoot-out with these undesirables, but that wouldn't save The Shelter, goddammit.''

Feeling a new swoop of dread, April demanded, "What do you mean?"

"I mean, if we capture these yahoos and take them to prison, they're going to tell the world about this place. It won't be safe as a safe house anymore.''

"You aren't suggesting that we have to *kill* them?" Semi said.

"Much as I'd like to—" Hack gave Ivan a sidelong, supplicating look. "No.''

April stepped forward to rest the gunstock on the tabletop. Staring at the ugly gray barrel, she thought there must be a better weapon against men so ignorant that they solved every problem with violence.

Semi's hand slipped around the nape of her neck. Its warmth sent a shiver down her back. She should be marrying him right now! If for no other reason, she was determined to outsmart the lowlifes who had interrupted her wedding.

"Have these guys seen Clint here, do you think?" she asked Ivan. "Did they follow you from the bus station?"

"No way. We weren't followed.''

"So probably they're here because they received information from—somewhere—that Clint was here?"

Ivan shrugged, not sure of her point.

"If they haven't seen him, we can trick them into thinking they have the wrong address. Then The Shelter can still be a safe house.''

Everyone except Gayner looked skeptical. He said, "Yeah. We can act like this is a rehab place and we're all druggies getting clean.''

"We don't have to act like anything," Semi said. "We're just two families about to have a wedding.''

"But the wedding scenario wouldn't account for our

guns. I don't want to face these guys unarmed," Ivan protested.

April bit her lip against saying anything about shotgun weddings.

"Besides," Ivan added, "if they've been here very long, they may have seen Hack patrolling."

"Five minutes is almost up," Dale warned quietly.

A thud from the direction of the front hall put Ivan's revolver into his hand and backed everyone else up two steps. A moment later, Clint loomed in the doorway, grinning gamely, though his forehead was as sweaty as if the house were forty degrees warmer.

"I'll pay for the door," he told Hack. "Ivan shouldn't have locked me in. I'll go talk to those guys outside. I sent for them."

"You did what?" Ivan's voice was a few notches short of a scream, and April could feel her own eyes stretching in the same horrified expression as his. "Are you insane?"

"Five minutes is too long," Buck complained, lapping his overcoat tighter across his chest.

"Nah. You just got no finesse," Dusty said, bending his face to the match between his hands, savoring that first delicious tang of tobacco when the cigarette caught. "Five minutes isn't long enough. It's the best part of an operation like this—the looking-forward-to, you know? Like waiting for a party to start. Or like—" He gazed off into the star-spangled sky, on the verge of revelation. "Like foreplay. Know what I mean?"

Buck didn't, so he grunted.

"We got all night," Dusty said, nudging his buddy with a vigorous elbow. "Enjoy."

Buck grunted again.

"Up there's the Big Dipper," Dusty pointed out. "This is great, isn't it? Being out here in the country with all this fresh air?" he said past the smoldering cigarette. "We'll give 'em another five minutes."

"This running and hiding's not for me," Clint was saying. "The boys will let me back. I got close to fifty thousand dollars in a safety deposit box I been saving up. I'll buy my way back with that. They'll beat me up first, I guess."

"They'll kill you, you pea-brain," Ivan said.

"You invited these hit men out here?" April's outrage shook her voice. "*You* turned my wedding night into a running firefight?" Ignoring Semi's hand trying to pat calmness into her arm, she snarled, "Well, I'm not surrendering. *You* aren't surrendering."

"It's been more than five minutes," Dale announced, anguish in her soft voice.

Hack waved an accusatory finger at April. "You've got a plan? Let's hear it."

He'd never asked for her advice before. That alone made her determined to think of something.

"Ivan, you take Clint back to your room," April ordered. "Stay with him. If our front line out here fails, you can come out shooting."

Getting a nod from Hack, Ivan pushed Clint down the hall. "Next time you get homesick, Ajax, just suck your thumb for a while."

Not a safe house, April thought fiercely, looking around the motley group, trying to see it as strangers would: a boy, his eyes wild with the threat and the promise of fears to come. An ancient giant, his eyes glowing just as ambivalently. Two short women, one in a scruffy brown coat with peanut butter on a sleeve and one with a green stain drooling down the front of her white blouse, both women rubbing dust off the trestle table with their bare fingers.

192 / CAROL CAIL

"A madhouse," April said, shaking her head rue-fully. "That's what we look like."

There was a gentle wave of nervous, tittering comment, cut off by new crashes from the kitchen. Someone was breaking down the backdoor.

Reaching for the shotgun, Hack said urgently, "Time's up, so madhouse it is. April and Semi, you're the keepers. The rest of us are inmates." He slid the gun into the space below the tabletop where a leaf would ordinarily be stored.

One last splintering crash came from the kitchen. A moment later, someone rapped with deceptive gentleness on the dining room door.

Twisting to look at Semi, April whispered, "I love you." His hand tightened on her arm.

She wanted to tell her grandfather the same thing, but she knew he would consider it a weakness caused by fear.

When Semi let go of her, stepped away, and drew a breath to speak to their tormentors, she felt the sudden, awful helplessness of terror. They were all going to die, swept by machine-gun bullets, their blood painting the walls to sicken and disgust whoever would eventually find them.

"What do you want?" Semi shouted, his voice as strong and dear as it had ever been. "Who are you to burst into our house in the middle of the night?"

"Just open up," was the bored answer. "We're getting tired of doing it the hard way."

Semi scanned everyone with a reassuring look that included a wink at Gayner, who, now that the violence was a room's length away, had become less avid about it.

"How do we act?" Wanda whispered.

"Do what comes naturally," was Semi's less-than-kind answer before he unlocked and threw open the door.

Two faces as hard and cold as cement slabs peered in at them. The front face said, "You didn't send us Clint."

"We didn't have a Clint to send you," Semi said, folding his arms and giving every appearance of being at ease. "We don't have a Clint."

"Oh, we don't," the same man mocked, stepping into the room, waggling his gun to be sure everyone had seen it.

The second man filled the doorway, his pistol also out and ready, his eyes as bored as if this were a duty call on distant, disliked relatives.

"Please put those weapons away," April said severely. "You're frightening our residents. Just breaking the window was enough to send some of them into hysterics." She glanced meaningfully at Dale, who obliged with a howl that jerked the second man's eyes wide open.

Patsy, too, began to cry—real tears that shimmered on her red face. "I should have gone home. Oh-oh-oh, I want to go home!"

April strode around the table to put her arms around Patsy and to put herself closer to the trigger end of the hidden shotgun. "If you men don't go at once, we may have a riot on our hands here. Our patients aren't used to this much excitement."

"Patients?" Number One echoed.

"Cut the crap and give us Clint," Number Two mumbled.

It gave April great satisfaction to think of them as Number One and Number Two. Out loud, she said, "You—gentlemen—don't seem to know where you are."

"The Shelter. For the mentally disturbed." Semi

helped her lie. "Of central Ohio." He smiled his smile. "Incorporated."

"A loony bin?" Number One said, suspicion darkening his eyes.

"Not a loony bin," April corrected him crisply. "A home for the socially impaired."

"Uh-huh. Who's in charge here?"

"I am," April and Semi said in stereo.

"You two are okay and the rest are all bonkers?"

"That's a crude way to put it," April answered coldly. "But—yes."

"So how come everybody's dressed up?" Number One said, skepticism apparent in his voice and his grin.

"We're celebrating New Year's Eve." April spread her arms and let them drop to her sides, implying exasperation at the question.

"It ain't New Year's Eve." Number Two caught her out with a sneer.

"These people don't know that," Semi said. "They don't even know what year it is."

Snickering, Number One turned to Number Two. "You buy this story?"

Number Two shrugged.

"Me neither."

Wanda screeched her chair backward and stood. "Young man, your aura is a sight. All blotchy black riddled with slime green." She sat down again with a thump and began to chant, Indian-style. April caught the words "hickory dickory."

"Oh, the shame, the shame, the shame," Dale contributed at the top of her lungs.

William began to giggle. Gayner held his crotch and whined, very realistically, about peeing.

"Shut up! Everybody shut up!" Number One screamed. Everyone stopped, holding his or her breath. "What's wrong with him?" he said, pointing at Hack.

The old man was leaning against the wall, loose-limbed, slack-jawed. He'd even managed to drool down his chin. April had the irrational impulse to applaud.

Instead, she said, "Manic-depressive. One minute he's like this, and the next he's running around the place with a toy rifle, swearing to kill the bastards."

"Better watch out, Buck," Number One joked. Buck, aka Number Two, didn't laugh.

For a moment the room was so quiet they could hear the lilac bush by the kitchen porch rattling its dry limbs. April willed the men to believe her, give it up, go away. She could feel seven other minds joining her in that single thought.

Number One rippled his shoulders and cleared his throat. "We'll have to search the place. Starting—" He strolled to the door between the dining room and the hall, cautiously cracked it ajar, and peered through, one palm mock-shading his eyes. "Starting this way."

The collective sigh of dismay was quickly converted into manic activity. Wanda pounded the table and sang the alphabet. William performed a one-man laugh track. Patsy doubled over, hyperventilating. Dale, who had surreptitiously smeared her red lipstick into a clown's mouth, grimaced, displaying equally red teeth.

Gayner's shrill voice overrode them all. "If I can't go to the bathroom, I'm going to do it in my pants."

"Oh, dear." April shouted at Number One. "He will, too. We're just getting him potty-trained."

"Okay, Okay! Go," the man ordered Gayner, waving him out with the pistol.

Gayner sprinted through the hall door and away. April was startled to see him slide to a stop at Ivan's door and let himself in.

She nodded at Number One. "He'll be in there a while. Bodily functions fascinate him."

"Buck, you watch this snake pit while the keeperess

here shows me around the house." Number One mock-bowed to April and offered his arm.

Not taking it, she said, "You don't know what you're saying. This is a huge place."

"We're in no hurry. We got all night."

"If you're determined to do this," Semi said, "I'll show you the house. April, you sit down."

Number One jutted his jaw. "April, you start walking. I'm giving the orders, and I pick you to give me the tour." He emphasized his point with an impatient yank of her wrist.

"Hey," Semi said.

"Come on, then," April interrupted, already striding toward the hall before Semi could commit any dangerous heroics.

Number One had to scurry to catch up.

Her bravery wasn't all an act. She had, after all, bested Ralph Greene just hours before. She could best this equally vacuous barbarian as well.

He grabbed her arm before she could bypass Ivan's room. "This is the bathroom where the kid went, right?" He tilted his head to listen at the door.

April also leaned toward the door and carelessly yelled next to his ear, "Are you okay, Gayner?"

"I'm throwing up," was the muffled answer. The groaning and retching that followed would have worried April if she hadn't heard Gayner's prowess with sound effects before.

She held her breath, not needing Superman's X-ray vision to know that Ivan waited on the other side of the wooden barrier, revolver at the ready. When Number One tapped her on the shoulder and waved his pistol for her to move on, she kept her face carefully blank of the relief she felt. Clever, clever, Gayner! Thanks to him, Ivan and Clint were still a secret.

Bustling along the hall, she indicated the door to

Clint's bedroom and announced, "This is William and Gayner's room."

"How'd it get staved in like that?"

Clint had, indeed, put a splintery porthole at shoulder height.

"That's just an example of why our clients are here," April said. "William has no patience whatsoever with a door that sticks."

Grunting, Number One tried to wrestle the sagging door across its sill.

Don't let him recognize Clint's smell, the black suit in the closet, the inevitable flotsam of underwear, April petitioned whatever gods might be attending.

Apparently Number One had no patience for sticking doors either. After one hearty kick, he gave up and peeked through the two-inch crack for all of a second before motioning April to move along.

Thank you, thank you, thank you.

"This next door might be locked," she said, remembering that she'd been unable to open it earlier in the day. "It's Wanda and Patsy's room, and they have this paranoia that someone's going to steal their belongings."

This time the door swung open easily, and what had been Sherry's bedroom was revealed in all its bareness.

"Not that they have anything to steal!" April hastened to add.

Number One frowned. "One single bed and a crib?"

"Yes, well, you see, Patsy won't sleep anywhere except in a baby's bed. She just fits, curled up in a fetal position."

Shaking his head, Number One muttered, "This is crazy."

April pushed past him and continued up the hall. "Mister, that's what we've been trying to tell you."

*   *   *

Semi said, "These poor people can't hurt you. Why don't you put your gun away?" He hoped his smile was disarming, and then smiled more broadly at the unspoken pun.

Buck glowered and straightened taller, resting the pistol across his chest, more ready than before.

Semi looked down and his eyes fixed on Wanda, sitting with her back to him. His mother's frowzy hair and frail stock of neck above the derelict tan coat sent a wave of tenderness through him. He wanted to kneel and take her in his arms and thank her for everything she'd done for him; he could even forgive her for his name.

"I'm thirsty," she said in her crisp, determined way. "Patsy, let's go get some milk."

Semi touched her gently on the shoulder, not sure he should encourage whatever was on her mind.

Patsy, too, looked less than enthusiastic about making any sudden moves. "Can't someone else get it?"

"No," Wanda said. "You and me." She flattened both hands on the table, ready to stand up.

"Uhh, I don't think you ought to leave the room," Buck said, leaning back to peer up the hall. His buddy and April had disappeared. "You'll have to wait for your milk."

As if suddenly struck deaf, Wanda stood up and marched toward the kitchen. "Come on, Patsy. We'll put chocolate syrup in it."

Whimpering, Patsy raised her eyebrows at Semi. He bustled over to her and helped her up. "Just milk, ladies," he said, walking them toward the kitchen door, keeping himself between them and Buck, who had taken a halfhearted step in their direction. The women scuttled into the kitchen and Wanda came back to grasp the doorknob and shut the door, her face as expressionless as a sleepwalker's.

Semi had no idea what Wanda had in mind—very probably she was thirsty and wanted a drink of milk.

To Buck, he said, "They'll be right back. They can't hurt anything. Better to let them have their milk than risk one of their fits."

Buck rocked back on his heels, his expression as blankly wary as that of a water buffalo sensing predators.

Everyone in the dining room settled into an attitude of bored waiting. Whatever was going on in the kitchen or in Clint's room or on April's guided tour, nothing was audible. The loudest sound was Buck's congested breathing. Semi's eyes caught Hack's for one flicker of commiserating recognition.

And always, in the back of Semi's mind, April floated just out of his reach. That he couldn't take her hand right now and lead her to safety was almost intolerable. He wasn't sure how long he could stand the anguish of this feeling of impotence before he began howling like the craziest of them all.

"If this is an insane asylum, how come you don't have a fence around the grounds?"

"I told you, we're just starting up. That's why most of these rooms are still empty." April stamped upstairs ahead of Number One. She rubbed her arms, longing for a coat. "Since we have only a handful of residents, it's easy to keep an eye on all of them till the fence is installed."

"Clint!" the goon shouted and forced April to a stop while he listened. "Christ," he complained, walking again, "this place is a monstrosity. He could be anywhere. Basement. Attic. Something tells me this is a big waste of time."

"*I'm* telling you it's a big waste of time. Why don't

you believe me? There is nobody named Clint in this house.''

All the little ivory fibs she'd told from childhood to the present moment *must* have been good practice for this one life-or-death lie. Mentally vowing that if successful now, she would retire from lying forever, April stepped in front of him, bringing them both to a halt.

Showing him her unwavering eyes, she repeated, "There is nobody named Clint in this house." Her jaw set, she kept staring, like a hypnotist with a recalcitrant subject.

He stared back. "How about if I believe you, and instead of looking over the rest of this museum, we go into one of these bedrooms and I'll look *you* over?"

It was such a clumsy imitation of bad movie dialogue, April felt more like laughing than screaming. Granted, he held her life in his beefy hand. She ought to cringe and grovel some, to lull him further into thinking he had everything under control. But damned if she would. His threats, like Ralph's earlier, made her fighting mad.

And so, while Number One grinned like a cat smelling something interesting, she recklessly stuck her finger down her throat in a first-class performance of outgagging Gayner.

TWELVE

"Hey, you in the kitchen," Buck raised his voice at the closed door. "Hurry it up." Turning to scowl at Semi, he added, "I don't hear anything."

"Drinking milk isn't all that noisy an activity," Semi pointed out.

Buck teetered from one foot to the other, obviously thinking more than was customary. "You," he said, motioning to Dale. "Go bring them back."

Smiling her lipstick-coated smile, she crossed to the door. Just before pulling it to her so she could step through, she called, "One, two, three on Wanda and Patsy. Here I come."

The door slammed in her wake, and again a hush fell over the room.

After perhaps one minute of listening and waiting, Buck began to swear under his breath.

"I'll get 'em for you," William volunteered, and he waltzed after Dale, hiccoughing giggles.

He danced through the door and reached back to haul it shut behind him. Too late it dawned on Buck where part of the problem lay, and his shout of "Leave that open" was overpowered by the slam.

Buck's worried look from Semi to Hack indicated he was counting his remaining prisoners. "You," he said, pointing the pistol at Semi. "You and I are going into the kitchen, you first."

"All you milk lovers better drink fast," Semi called to warn them, his hand on the doorknob. "Mr. Buck and I are coming out there."

He paused before opening the door, hoping that his family had some trap awaiting Buck and also hoping that they didn't, since that would be horribly risky. Backing up and still holding onto the doorknob, Semi stepped on Buck's toe and felt the cold graze of the pistol on his neck.

Careful, everyone, he silently begged, stepping into the doorway.

A light was on—not the overhead fixture, but a dim fluorescent under a cabinet. William was standing a yard away, as if on his return trip to the dining room, a yellow-flowered glass in his hand.

Beckoning to Semi, he said, "You want some cow juice, too?"

Semi stepped over the threshold, saying, "No, I—" and bedlam broke loose. William, who had never touched Semi except with the gentle hand of brotherly-in-law love, twisted a fist into Semi's shirtfront and yanked him sideways, at the same time shouting like Miss Piggy.

Startled, Buck froze with one foot in the kitchen, but only for a moment. William straight-armed his glass, sloshing whatever was in it into Buck's wide eyes. At the same time Patsy, who was standing on a chair at one side of the door, smashed a rolling pin against Buck's left temple, and Dale, atop a chair on the other side, rang a rusty cast-iron skillet against his right ear. William leaped out of the path of Wanda's fireplace poker as it whistled through the air and depressed Buck's solar plexus.

Like executioners at a condemned man's dispatch, they couldn't know which blow was the one that dropped Buck. He hit the floor so hard, dust puffed up.

Semi detached the gun from the unconscious man's hand and gingerly reached it out to Hack, who had shoved away from the wall to catch the end of the excitement. Past the old man's shoulder, Semi noticed Ivan's door ease open and Ivan peep out. Making a circle of his thumb and forefinger, Semi waved him back inside.

Hack, stroking his white stubbled chin, gazed down at their catch. "Now what?"

"Now I'm going to go find April before that SOB who's got her does something dumb," Semi muttered as renewed fear for her arced through him.

"No, wait." Hack grabbed his arm. "We've got 'em on the ropes now. Let's think before we throw another punch."

"What if there's more like him outside?" Dale asked quietly.

"There aren't," Semi said, surprised at how much he wanted to spit on the prostrate Buck. "They thought this would be a snap course, right, Hack?"

Hack's hand tightened and gave Semi's arm a shake that meant either affection or palsy. "You'll do, son. I'm mighty glad April Lynn hired you. Fact, when we got more time, I'd like to discuss hiring you myself. A guidance counselor would give this safe-house operation some class."

The words didn't register. All Semi could think of was getting April back, making her safe.

"I've got an idea," he said, clenching his jaw.

*   *   *

"Cute, cute," Number One growled at April's defiant finger-in-the-throat. "Real cute." He shoved her ahead of him along the upstairs hall.

It was lonesome up here, away from the moral support of Semi and Hack and the rest. She had started out eager to draw the danger away from the others, but in this cold, echoing part of the house, her bravado flagged.

Of all the rooms in The Shelter, the one April hated the most to reveal to this creep's beady eyes was the blue room with its bridal bed invitingly turned down. Pretending to be preoccupied with pointing out a badly faded reproduction of *Sunflowers* on the opposite side of the hall, she sailed past the blue room door.

He didn't fall for it. "Hold it. Let's see this one."

Switching on the light, he whistled. "Nice layout. Whose is this? Not one of the locos', I bet."

"Our doctor's. When he comes long enough to spend the night."

"He's not here now."

"Obviously." She tried to walk on down the hall.

Number One stuck out his log of an arm to block the way. "What's this doctor's name?"

Eager to end the tour and be back in the same room with Semi, she blurted the first thing that came to mind. "Who."

"The doctor."

"I told you. Dr. Who." Seeing his expression settle into the lazy-lidded squint of an angry alligator, she hastened to amend the name. "Dr. Hu. H-U. It's Chinese."

"Humpf." he continued to give her the reptilian look, his bulk barricading her against the wall. Then he snorted and laughed cigarette breath at her. "You're cute, you know it?"

He crowded closer, bracing himself around her with

both hands on the wall. She was, literally, between a rock and a hard place.

Her anger, which had been humming just below the surface, suddenly choked to a stop, and fright rushed in to fill the void. Who was stupid now? Instead of carelessly congratulating herself on her superiority, instead of baiting this vermin, she should have been bowing and nodding and calling him "Sir."

She might be tall enough to look him in the eye, but she wasn't strong or mean enough to win a physical fight.

"What was that?" she said in a feeble attempt to regain the lead in mental acuity.

"I didn't hear nothing." The hand without the gun cupped her chin as gently as any lover could have wished.

"Well, I did. Sounded like your friend. Buck. Bellowing."

For a suspenseful second, Number One balanced on the decision fence between business and pleasure. Then, with a sigh, he tipped over onto the sensible side.

"All right, honey. Let's go see what the big doofus wants. Whaddaya bet he's found Clint?"

April led off back the way they'd come, as fast as her high heels would wobble her.

"Phew. What was in that glass?" Semi said, breathing through his mouth to avoid the smell of Buck's wet shirt as he dragged Buck to the fireplace.

"Some of Patsy's cleaning ammonia." William squatted beside Buck's head and pried apart each reddening eyelid. "Dale, bring me some tap water to flush it out."

"Hurry," Hack said, backing to the nearest chair

and easing down in it. He looked his age and maybe a few months more.

"This is certainly, definitely, absolutely, positively my last day here," Patsy announced as Semi strode past her toward the dining room.

Number One let April lead him along the route they'd come. Along the hall, down the wide, gritty marble stairs, into the front entry, around and under the stairs into the central hall—April's teeth rivaled her clacking high heels as cold and apprehension coursed through her.

At the far end of the hall, the dining room door stood open as before. Through its frame she could see Semi, Wanda, and half of William—all three sitting at the trestle table, hands clasped on it, shoulders slumped, looking bored by waiting. Hearing her coming, Semi turned his head and smiled, melting some of the ice in her center.

Each step closer to that smile made her feel one degree happier. Grinning back at him, she fairly flew.

"Hold it!" Number One commanded. "We didn't see the bathroom."

"Bathroom?" She slowed without stopping.

"I said, 'Hold it!' " he snarled, snagging her sleeve in his fist. Something popped before she successfully twitched herself loose. Like a well-tuned motor, her anger fired up and began to idle again.

"This is a new dress," she complained, finger-testing the damaged shoulder seam.

"Open this," Number One said, indicating Ivan's door.

"Gayner's probably still—"

He reached in front of her and wrenched the knob around. The door drifted inward on a dark room. As Number One stretched inside and patted the wall till the overhead fixture snapped on, April's hand leaped to her mouth to trap her gasp of apprehension.

There was the bed, the bureau, the open closet door. No counterfeit money, no stacks of how-to books for beginning outlaws. No Gayner, no Ivan, no Clint.

Looking sidelong at the crack between door and jamb, April could see no hint of bodies pressed to the wall hiding.

"You said this was a bathroom." Number One sounded shocked. "This ain't a bathroom."

"I didn't say it was a bathroom. You just jumped to that conclusion, I guess."

"The kid came in here to pee and throw up!"

Leaning forward, she lowered her voice. "What kind of room it is doesn't make much difference to Gayner."

Number One backed out hastily and slammed the door.

"Hello," Semi called from the dining room. "Welcome back." He stood up to meet April in the doorway, enclosing her icy hands in his two warm ones.

Crowding past them, Number One swept the room with a surprised gaze. "Where's Buck?" He went to the kitchen door and yanked it open. "Buck!"

Giving the silence all of five seconds, he twisted around to study the assembled group again. April, also wondering what had happened to Buck, helped him look from face to face: Wanda, humming what sounded like "Taps." William, counting his fingers. Dale, her mouth like the muzzle of a lion with a fresh kill. Patsy, her cheeks pink as with a fever. Gayner, turning his eyelids inside out. Hack, in the same catatonic slouch as before. Semi.

Semi, his left hand still tight around her right, telepathing courage, hope, love—*pain*, if he didn't lighten up.

"Your friend is out there in the kitchen," Semi said. "With the doctor."

"Show me," Number One commanded.

Keeping April's hand in his, Semi towed her gently past the mobster and over the kitchen threshold.

By the pulsing light of a cabinet fluorescent, April could see that someone had tacked decaying quilts over the broken windows. They sucked slowly in and out as if the house were breathing, and a fire pulsed in the fireplace.

At that warm end of the room, on another quilt, Buck's enormous shoe soles formed a V while the rest of him mounded like a D on its back. The man leaning over him, listening to his chest with a stethoscope, was Ivan.

Jostling April out of his way, Number One rushed to get a better view. "What's going on here? What happened to him?"

Frowning, Ivan waved for silence while he hopped the stethoscope three inches down and two inches back. Sighing, he spread the ear tips clear of his head and dropped them around his neck. He was wearing black slacks, a navy jacket, a purple shirt, and brown socks. And no shoulder holster. April imagined any doctor in a hurry might dress like this.

"He's going to be fine," Ivan intoned. "Just had a bump on the head. He'll come to shortly."

"Who slugged him?" Number One swung around to narrow his eyes at Semi. "Someone's going to be sorry for this."

"Mister, uhh, you're jumping to conclusions." Ivan raised his voice. "If you'll look here, I'll explain your friend's injuries to you."

Lower lip jutting, Number One bent over, hands on knees, the forgotten gun pointing at Buck's belt buckle. "This better be the truth, pal. And say—" He temporarily straightened. "Where were you when we broke in?"

"On the road. Just arrived ten minutes ago."

Number One wrinkled his nose. "What stinks?"

"I didn't have any smelling salts, so we've been trying to bring him around with ammonia. Now, see here, this bruise?" Ivan pointed at Buck's left temple.

"Yeah," Number One conceded. He glanced uneasily at Ivan's face and was again momentarily distracted. "You don't look Chinese."

Frowning, Ivan bulldogged on. "And on the other side of his head here, another bruise."

"Yeah?" Number One twisted around to glare at Semi and April. "Who did it?"

"Not 'who,' " Ivan said. "What."

"What. What?"

"You want to show this gentleman where his friend fell?" Ivan asked Semi, folding up the stethoscope and inserting it into a squat black bag on his far side.

Semi backed up, beckoning to Number One. "It was a freak accident. We'd all come out here to the refrigerator to get some refreshments—"

"You'd what?" came the roar of disbelief. "What is this—some kind of bleeping party?"

"And since people were a little stirred up," Semi went on, "by your—misguided—visit, they behaved rather childishly, I'm sorry to say."

"Childish—"

"Your friend was laid low by"—Semi touched his fingers to an eye, signaling embarrassment—"a food fight."

Number One's mouth worked; his voice didn't.

Semi rushed to finish the explanation. "William threw milk at Dale and Dale threw milk at Patsy and so on, and they just got carried away and threw some into Buck's face, too. He was so startled and understandably angered that he threw himself at William, slipped on a puddle of milk, and fell. Right here.'' Semi indicated the L where the cabinet met the wall beside the dining room door. "He just skidded headfirst into that spot there. Like a jet overshooting the runway.''

In spite of the circumstances, April ached to laugh.

Number One, obviously not sharing her amusement, began to mutter sibilantly. His swearing gathered speed and volume.

To avoid hearing individual words, April deliberated about where Ivan's gun was. Under his knee? In the black bag? She could visualize Hack waiting just out of sight inside the dining room now, his shotgun slanted at the ready across his chest.

Number One's tirade slowed to a smattering of "damns." Prowling back to his comatose buddy, he nudged Buck's hip with a less-than-solicitous toe. To Ivan, he said, "You better hope he remembers it the same way when he wakes up.'

Ivan nodded. "He will. Although he'll undoubtedly experience some confusion due to the concussion. You might want to hospitalize him for observation. Shall I help you get him to your car?''

For longer than April could hold her breath, Number One stood there considering. Finally he hunkered down and tapped Ivan's chest with the gun barrel to emphasize key words. "Bring him *around*. I want to hear the story from *him*. *Then* we're out of here.''

"Hand me that ammonia bottle again," Ivan called carelessly over his shoulder to Semi.

April trailed after Semi, unwilling to allow so much as a room's width between them.

"One side effect of a blow to the head is burning, blurred vision,'' Ivan advised, swiping the open bottle under Buck's nose. "I'm sure he'll complain about that."

"If it happened like you claim, he deserves every side effect he gets," Number One grumbled. "Letting a handful of loop-de-loops drop him."

"Sorry, this stuff doesn't seem to be getting through to him," Ivan said. "You'd better get him to a hosp—"

"Uhhh," Buck said. His bloodshot eyes flapped open. Repeating the groan, he struggled to sit up.

In his best floorside manner, Ivan supported Buck's arm and counseled, "Take it easy, fella. You'll be okay. You just took a nasty header on a slippery—"

"Shut up!" Number One bleated. Pushing his face inches from Buck's, he said, "What happened to you?"

"Uhh, I, uhh, took a nasty—header on a—slippery—" He faltered, waiting for the next clue.

"You remember William throwing milk at you?" Ivan obliged.

"Oh. Oh, yeah. I remember him throwing—" Buck's forehead wrinkled doubtfully.

"And then you fell," Ivan rushed on smoothly.

"Yeah, I guess so."

"Stop coaching him, damn it." Number One smacked Buck's shoulder with the flat of one hand. "Think about it, dummy. Who knocked you out? William?"

"Naw. He was way off in front of me."

"That guy?" Number One's accusatory finger aimed at Semi.

"Uh-unh. He was in front of me, too."

"Who, then? One of the women?"

"Aw, no. They couldn't of knocked me out."

"Well, how do you explain it?" Number One literally spit at him. "How in the world of common sense does your excuse of a brain account for keeling over in a wimpy stupor—stupid?"

This is it, April thought, planting her toes like a tennis player and getting ready to throw herself in front of Semi.

Buck's confused expression solidified into cold resentfulness. Knocking away Ivan's supporting hand, he shook off, too, the role of victim. With a straightened back and stiffened shoulders, he gave his partner a look so evil, it should have required an antidote.

"I slipped and hit my head," he said. "Let's get the hell out of this fruit bin. I bet Clint's in the next county wetting his pants laughing about sending us here."

"However did you think of protecting Clint and Ivan's hiding place like that, Gayner?" April was hugging him in spite of his yelps to be set free.

"From the drug busts," he said, resigning himself to stand still and be mortified. "My mom's friends would hide the stuff in one room and then move it to a room the cops had searched already. Except the narcs were too smart to fall for it."

After the initial celebration over Buck and Number One's departure—a departure Ivan had confirmed by following them to the interstate—cleanup began. Since Hack didn't have any more sheets of plywood, William and Semi took down two bedroom doors to nail over the ruined kitchen windows. Patsy and Wanda vied to see who could sweep up the most glass in the longest time. Dale, having scrubbed her face, began brewing coffee the color of bituminous coal. The cats, who'd disappeared during the melee, began to return, stiff-legged and wary.

April folded the quilts that had served as makeshift window covering. She picked up the one that had been Buck's pallet.

"Where'd Ivan get a doctor's bag for the occasion?" she asked, poking the black satchel with her shoe.

"It's his safecracking tools," Hack said as he dumped a log on the fire. "Stethoscope and all."

Laughing, April bent down to pry open the sides. "Good thing Buck didn't need more intensive care. There's a screwdriver and an electric drill in here."

"Oh, hell," Hack said, sounding more weary than disgusted. "I suppose we ought to go let Clint loose."

"Where is he? I can do it."

"Tied up in Sherry's closet."

As she passed behind Semi, who was holding a door in place while William hammered it to the window frame, April patted his bottom. Pausing, thinking how nice that felt, she backed up and patted him again.

"Are we married yet?" she whispered at his ear.

"No. And not having fun yet, either," he answered. "Soon, though. On both counts. I can hardly wait to—"

William's renewed hammering left the rest to April's imagination.

Slipping through the dining room, an obstacle course of scattered chairs, she walked to what had been Sherry's room.

"Wake up, Clint," she sang out, crossing to the closed closet door. "Rise and shine." She opened the door a foot and peered in warily, feeling like a zoo keeper instructed to bring out the gorilla.

He was sitting on the floor, knees to his chest, hands behind his back, a red paisley handkerchief tied between his teeth. Leaning into the stuffy, dim space, April picked at the knot in the cloth securing his bare feet. It soon became clear why they were bare—the cloth proved to be one black nylon sock, and the mate to it was tied around Clint's wrists. She nudged him around to work on the second sock.

"You almost got us all killed, I hope you realize," she scolded, nervous to be in such intimate proximity to an honest-to-gosh bad guy. "It's going to take me a while to forgive you for nearly ruining my wedding. I'm sure not going to throw the bouquet in your direction."

As his hands twisted free, she scrambled up and out of reach. He could damn well undo the gag himself.

"Missus Jones," he spluttered inaccurately as she was turning the corner into the hall.

She leaned her head back, one foot still poised for the next step, and frowned at him. "What?"

"Are Dusty and Buck gone?"

"Yeah."

His eyes closed down to ugly slits. "They gave up that easy? What a pair of rabbits. They got no more hustle than that, to hell with them. They deserve my roo-rahing to the Feds. Do I know how to *rat*? Do *I* know how—"

April wasn't listening anymore. She was rushing back to the kitchen, calling ahead, "Let's get this wedding on the road!"

William's voice was deep and resonant. "Like two drops of rain in a quiet pool, you are April, you are Semi, and you both are the amorphous water. Separate. Not separate. Equal."

Out of the side of her shining right eye, April could see Hack. He had walked her into the parlor, patted Semi's shoulder, and said, "She's all yours, son." Now her grandfather slumped in a wingback chair, his face more serenely tired than she had ever noticed it.

Semi was promising to let her be herself, alone but never lonely. "I'll respect you, April, and I'll work for your respect." He stopped to draw a long breath, his signature smile beginning to light his eyes. "Is that enough?" he stage-whispered.

"Enough," she said. "It's far more than I ever dreamed or deserved."

Between Semi's and William's padded shoulders, April could see Wanda's expectant face. The little woman looked as alert and cheerful as if it were the beginning of a normal day instead of the ending of a most abnormal one.

"April," William coached, "what do you promise to Semi?"

She smiled at the man who was halfway to being her husband. "Before you came into my life, I thought I was content. *Now* I am content."

Behind her, either Ivan or Patsy sighed.

"I promise to be faithful to you."

Beyond Semi's ramrod back, Dale stretched forward from the piano bench and put a gentle hand on Gayner's elbow to moor the boy's invisible-basketball dribbling.

"I won't ever knowingly hurt you. Thank you for changing my future, for letting me be with you, for teaching me to love."

The room and the spectators faded into the distance as April stared into Semi's cherishing eyes. Whatever else she wanted to say, she would tell him in private. Not waiting to be prompted, she swayed forward to kiss the groom.

Demonstrating considerable willpower, they stepped apart and beamed around the room.

"God bless," William said.

"Yippee!" Dale exclaimed, jumping off the piano stool to give them a joint bear hug.

Accepting embraces and wishes and kisses, April knuckled moisture from under one eye and smiled till her mouth felt a size bigger. The mantel clock chimed twice, touching off a yawning epidemic.

"Patsy, rustle these people something to eat before

you show them to their beds,'' Hack said, trying to free himself from the depths of the overstuffed chair.

Wanda rolled up her coat sleeves, ready to help. ''Swinburne, I don't think you've ever said how it was that you and April met.''

''She dropped in at my office,'' he said, eyeing his bride with amusement. ''Thinking it was a dating service.''

''I did not! I was trying to find—'' She snapped her mouth shut, glanced guiltily at Hack, and ended the sentence with ''A job.'' Remembering that she had, under the duress of Number One's threats, promised herself not to lie anymore, she added, ''For someone else.''

''Do we get to throw rice?'' Gayner piped up, dancing backward into the hall ahead of the crowd.

Patsy said, ''Haven't got any.''

''Birdseed is good,'' Wanda said. ''But that's if the bridal couple is outside.''

''We could run around the house once,'' Semi offered. To April, he warned, ''Watch they don't tie tin cans to your shoes.''

Laughing, April turned toward her grandfather and discovered he'd never made it to his feet. Hands on his knees, elbows cocked, he daydreamed at the floor.

''You okay, Hack?'' April asked, releasing Semi's arm to kneel beside the old man and study his face.

Everyone else had clumped into the hall; the footfalls and voices dwindled into nothing.

'' 'Course I'm all right,'' Hack snarled. ''Just because I been threatened by mafiosi and before that a wife beater come trespassing—just because I had to give my granddaughter away in marriage and it's five hours past my bedtime—just because I'll turn eighty-eight in ten skimpy months—why would I be tired?''

"Okay," she said, lightly snapping his suspender strap. "Hey, I'm married. So are you satisfied?"

"Half."

"Half!" She leaned away and peered at him as if sighting through the lower part of bifocals. "What do you mean half?"

Hack raised his eyes to Semi, who waited, a smile in place and his hands clasped behind his back, a consort prince patiently attending his queen.

Hack growled, "There's still the little matter of—" He planted both feet and stood to his full height, the better to squint belligerently down at April. "Great-grandchildren."

April groaned. Then she stood, too, the better to answer him straight-faced. "I'm sure Semi will rise to the task and help me come through."

Why ivory-lie when you can tell a tarnished truth?

EPILOGUE

The baby's face was turned in profile, one arm stretched over his head, his chubby knees flexed open like a frog. His gentle snoring swelled and deflated the blue-and-white-striped romper suit he wore.

April stood near the playpen, blending a rosy blob of paint on her palette, humming along to an Elton John song playing low on the radio. An Indian summer breeze filtered through the screen door of the north kitchen, which was now her studio.

Echoing footsteps announced someone's approach through the wooden-floored ballroom. Turning to motion for quiet to whoever appeared in the doorway, April saw that it was Millie Hamlin, one of the current "renters".

"Oh, isn't that a picture," Millie cooed, and then giggled into her hands at the realization that the living baby was, indeed, a picture on April's easel. "Can you come to the main kitchen now? We've got the cake and ice cream laid out, and your grandfather says he can spare ten minutes to celebrate his eighty-eighth birthday."

"Sounds like the day isn't making him feel any older," April said with her usual mixture of exasperation and pride for the old man. She dampened a rag with turpentine and rubbed at the specks on her fingers. "Would you mind staying with Jamie while I join the party?"

"Not at all." Millie sat down in the nearest kitchen chair and folded her hands. She still wore long-sleeved shirts to hide the bruises, but the country sun had tanned her face to a healthy glow, and she was smiling more often every day.

April shed Semi's white shirt that she'd appropriated for a paint smock since he didn't wear dress shirts very often anymore. "Thanks, Millie," she said, smoothing down the T-shirt underneath. "I'll send Jamie's mother to spell you in a few minutes."

April was passing through the parlor when she heard another pair of shoes coming along the main hall. She recognized these footsteps—shuffle, stride, stride, shuffle, hop, hop, hop.

"Hey, Mom!"

"Hey yourself."

"Patsy's got a smorgasbord laid out. You're gonna love it. Peanut butter and last night's chicken and catsup and potato chips and cucumbers and olives and birthday cake and ice cream."

"Yum. I'm coming."

"I'm supposed to tell everybody."

"Okay. Then I won't make you walk me to the feast."

It was just as well, Gayner's idea of walking being what it was. He swooped away down the hall, caroming back and forth off the walls, doubling the distance he had to go.

He'd started calling her "Mom" and Semi "Dad," not on the day the adoption papers were signed, but six months later, as if he wanted to give them a chance to change their minds.

April scratched at a spot of white she'd missed on her thumbnail. Turning the corner under the main staircase, she heard, one more time, someone coming toward her. These footsteps were dearly familiar, too, and she smiled in expectation.

Semi, in a blue denim work shirt and jeans, strode purposefully through the dining room. Seeing her, he stopped, filling the doorway. "Halt and pay tribute."

Bumping gently against him, she brushed her lips to his. He tasted salty-warm, and his skin smelled of fresh-cut grass.

She murmured against his prickly cheek, "Hack actually gave you time off from mowing to come to his party?"

"Not exactly. I ran out of gasoline, which is fortunate. I'd already run out of steam."

"Poor Semi. Would you rather be back in Dayton finding Gabe Meldon a job?" she teased, confident of his answer.

"No, but I know what I want you to give me for Christmas."

"A riding lawn mower?"

"A pack of goats."

"I don't think they're called—"

He began to kiss her to distraction. His strong arms started to coax her in the direction she'd already come.

"What are you doing?" she managed to say from under the pressure of his lips. "The party's back that way."

"We never got started on your plan to make love in every bedroom in the house," he mumbled against her cheek. "Remember you said we should do that?"

She pulled away to laugh. "I thought you were out

of steam. Besides, I'm painting Jamie Wager's portrait. I need to be back at the studio in about five minutes."

"Ha. That's plenty of time. I've done my part in less!"

Still laughing, she braced her feet. "No. You'll have to wait till tonight. Is that good enough?"

" 'Good' isn't the word for how it will be," Semi promised, stooping to stroke his mouth across her throat.

Then, before they moved apart to resume their walk toward the kitchen, he reverently spread both hands to touch the swell of life between them.

SHARE THE FUN . . .
SHARE YOUR NEW-FOUND TREASURE!!

You don't want to let your new books out of your sight? That's okay. Your friends can get their own. Order below.

No. 116 IVORY LIES by Carol Cail
April makes Semi a very unusual proposition and it backfires on them.

No. 89 JUST ONE KISS by Carole Dean
Michael is Nikki's guardian angel and too handsome for his own good.

No. 90 HOLD BACK THE NIGHT by Sandra Steffen
Shane is a man with a mission and ready for anything . . . except Starr.

No. 91 FIRST MATE by Susan Macias
It only takes a minute for Mac to see that Amy isn't so little anymore.

No. 92 TO LOVE AGAIN by Dana Lynn Hites
Cord thought just one kiss would be enough. But Honey proved him wrong!

No. 93 NO LIMIT TO LOVE by Kate Freiman
Lisa was called the "little boss" and Bruiser didn't like it one bit!

No. 94 SPECIAL EFFECTS by Jo Leigh
Catlin wouldn't fall for any tricks from Luke, the master of illusion.

No. 95 PURE INSTINCT by Ellen Fletcher
She tried but Amie couldn't forget Buck's strong arms and teasing lips.

No. 96 THERE IS A SEASON by Phyllis Houseman
The heat of the volcano rivaled the passion between Joshua and Beth.

No. 97 THE STILLMAN CURSE by Peggy Morse
Leandra thought revenge would be sweet. Todd had sweeter things in mind.

No. 98 BABY MAKES FIVE by Lacey Dancer
Cait could say 'no' to his business offer but not to Robert, the man.

No. 99 MOON SHOWERS by Laura Phillips
Both Sam and the historic Missouri home quickly won Hilary's heart.

No. 100 GARDEN OF FANTASY by Karen Rose Smith
If Beth wasn't careful, she'd fall into the arms of her enemy, Nash.

No. 101 HEARTSONG by Judi Lind
From the beginning, Matt knew Lainie wasn't a run-of-the-mill guest.

No. 102 SWEPT AWAY by Cay David
Sam was insufferable . . . and the most irresistible man Charlotte ever met.

No. 103 FOR THE THRILL by Janis Reams Hudson
Maggie hates cowboys, *all* cowboys! Alex has his work cut out for him.

No. 104 SWEET HARVEST by Lisa Ann Verge
Amanda never mixes business with pleasure but Garrick has other ideas.

No. 105 SARA'S FAMILY by Ann Justice
Harrison always gets his own way . . . until he meets stubborn Sara.

No. 106 TRAVELIN' MAN by Lois Faye Dyer
Josh needs a temporary bride. The ruse is over, can he let her go?

No. 107 STOLEN KISSES by Sally Falcon
In Jessie's search for Mr. Right, Trevor was definitely a wrong turn!

No. 108 IN YOUR DREAMS by Lynn Bulock
Meg's dreams become reality when Alex reappears in her peaceful life.

No. 109 HONOR'S PROMISE by Sharon Sala
Once Honor gave her word to Trace, there would be no turning back.

No. 110 BEGINNINGS by Laura Phillips
Abby had her future completely mapped out—until Matt showed up.

No. 111 CALIFORNIA MAN by Carole Dean
Quinn had the Midas touch in business but Emily was another story.

Meteor Publishing Corporation
Dept. 1192, P. O. Box 41820, Philadelphia, PA 19101-9828

Please send the books I've indicated below. Check or money order (U.S. Dollars only)—no cash, stamps or C.O.D.s (PA residents, add 6% sales tax). I am enclosing $2.95 plus 75¢ handling fee for *each* book ordered.

Total Amount Enclosed: $_____.

____ No. 116	____ No. 94	____ No. 100	____ No. 106
____ No. 89	____ No. 95	____ No. 101	____ No. 107
____ No. 90	____ No. 96	____ No. 102	____ No. 108
____ No. 91	____ No. 97	____ No. 103	____ No. 109
____ No. 92	____ No. 98	____ No. 104	____ No. 110
____ No. 93	____ No. 99	____ No. 105	____ No. 111

Please Print:
Name _____

Address _____ Apt. No. _____

City/State _____ Zip _____

Allow four to six weeks for delivery. Quantities limited.